FOOD FOR

In this nifty collection of Horror gems, the term "feeding frenzy" definitely takes on new meaning. "Share Alike" and "Fix Me Something to Eat" show us that our hosts and sometimes comrades are not always the pleasant folks we had thought them to be... "All of You" shows us just what an awful experience hungry little children can be. And speaking of children, "Yes, Burt, there is a Santa Claus" gives a new slant on the darker side of Old Saint Nick's true personality.

You may also find that affairs of the heart are not for the light hearted. "Sa'antha" and "Twice to Die" leave one wondering if the discovery of your soul mate is really all it's cracked up to be, and "Purdy's Circus" along with "The Mirror" put some serious doubts in the sanctity of marriage theory...

All in all this is a GREAT addition to our Horror Gems series and deserves to be read, revered and reviled by each and every horror fiend—dead or alive!

TABLE OF CONTENTS

HORROR GEMS

Volume 6
H. P. LOVECRAFT
and others

Compiled by Gregory Luce

ARMCHAIR FICTION
PO Box 4369, Medford, Oregon 97504

For more information about Armchair Books and products, visit our website at…

www.armchairfiction.com

Or email us at…

armchairfiction@yahoo.com

THE VIOLIN STRING

By Henry Hasse

Versatile Henry Hasse tries his hand—and most successfully—at modernizing a Lovecraft theme and a Lovecraft style to fashion an eerie tale of a man who was—or was not—mad.

THE MAN came silently, swiftly, approaching me out of the clustered shadows in the huge gloomy hall. I gave a start and rose from the chair. There was that indefinable feeling that I had been under scrutiny for some moments.

"You are the man from the magazine—" He said it not as a question. He stood poised, long arms hanging loose, the dark immobile face relieved only by an alertness about the eyes.

I nodded, reached for my credentials, but he stopped me with a gesture. "I know," he said. "You want to do the violin story. I showed Dr. Sherman your letter. He will be happy to receive you." A pause, and I felt the alert eyes upon me. "You are aware that others have tried?"

"I know that," I said brusquely. "And I know they were ill-equipped! Two years ago I covered the International Congress of Psychiatrists in London, and I heard Dr. Sherman give one of the outstanding addresses. I'm not after Sunday supplement stuff!"

"Ah-h-h," he said, and that was all. No censure of my bombastics, though his eyes showed it—or was that amusement?

He gestured, and I followed. Through a shadowy draped doorway, along another paneled hall redolent with brownish decay. It reminded me somehow of the stories of Lovecraft— but I cut those thoughts off abruptly.

"Here you are, sir." We had reached a room somewhere at the rear of the huge sprawling house. I was ushered in, I was announced, and the door closed softly behind me.

And Dr. Frederic Sherman—until lately one of the most renowned and respected figures in his field, whose brilliant career I had followed as a layman—this man rose to greet me with a hearty handshake. He professed to remember me! He even remarked on my excellent coverage of the International Congress!

I knew it was an improvised lie. I had put all of that in my letter. But I remembered him well, and now I wondered why I had expected to find him changed? For he hadn't changed at all—he was still tall and gaunt and vigorous, with heavy graying brows that seemed formidable, until you glimpsed the blue eyes peering and heard his jovial voice.

"So it's the story you want!" he boomed cheerfully. "I know. You think I don't remember you. But it's evident you must have heard, because you follow these things. You must be aware that I'm in disrepute now, eh?"

"Well," I hesitated, "let's just say, there are differing versions about this—this string from the violin..."

"Versions." His eyes clouded, then brightened as he looked at me. "Very well. When I have finished you'll believe. I'm going to relate the event exactly as it happened; more, I'll show you proof. The indisputable evidence!"

"Evidence!" I felt a sudden pulsing at my throat.

"Oh yes. I still have it, you know...the metal string, that damnable string! The string from the violin."

I didn't interrupt again, I dared not, as I accepted the chair he offered and settled down to listen.

IN MY profession (he began), I have had occasion to observe varying degrees of psychosis. Both those who were madmen in their genius, and quite conversely, geniuses who were madmen. Oh yes, there is a distinction! But as the years went by these cases lost their unusual aspects for me, and I remembered them only impersonally.

All save one. I refer, of course, to the case of Philip Maxton and the violin string. I assure you, there is no violation of professional ethics on my part in discussing it now.

I was residing then on Crescent Heights—you know the place?—and it was there that Maxton first came to me. It was March, and the sea was pounding. I recall that storm warnings had been out for most of the day. I had just settled down in my study, when there came a frantic ringing of the doorbell, and a minute later my servant ushered in the young man.

I tell you, sir, he was wild in appearance. Terror was upon him. He was about thirty, and I judged him to be a student, one whose quest might lie in the field of the true metaphysics. No, let me correct that! It's only that his name, when he introduced himself, was somewhat familiar to me. He was outstanding in that rather vague field of pseudo-science dealing with vibration and structural dimensions; he had also published some slight tracts on the latent powers of the mind, which I had read—for although some tended to be wild, others were of deep thought and possessed merit.

Philip Maxton. You know the name? Perhaps you even recall the stir that was roused by his disappearance.

He introduced himself in a rush of words. The first hints of the storm were on him, his clothes mud-spattered and damp. He shivered, but I could see it was *not* from the chill night.

"Come with me," I urged. "There's a fireplace in the next room where you can warm yourself—"

"A fireplace!" I'll never forget the way he uttered the word. There was *desire* in it, there was *despair* in it, and he looked at me through wild eyes. But in the next instant he became profuse in his thanks for what he called my kindness.

He refused to sit down. He stood away from the fire, stared at it with fascination. I studied him well as I filled my pipe. His outward expression baffled me. His attitude for the fire was almost one of primitive curiosity rather than gratitude for its warmth…and I noticed something else. He kept his head half turned away, cocked as though harking to something I was not meant to hear.

Outside, the storm broke with fury. I could hear it shrieking around the windows, lashing through the night as a smother of rain swept in from the bay.

"Fire," I murmured. "It fascinates you, does it not? So warm and soothing, and on a night like this—"

At my words, he began to shiver violently. I had gauged him well. He possessed an antipathy, even a fear of fire, albeit fire drew him irresistibly—a condition not too unusual even in normal people.

"Fire and storm," he uttered hollowly. "They possess me! They bring me to—*this*, and to things much worse!" He sought to control his trembling. "And yet I must seek fire and storm!"

"I'm sure you do," I said offhandedly, "and I'd like to hear about it. But we have the entire evening." So I dismissed it, and brought a measure of normalcy. "Tell me about *you*," I insisted.

It was what he waited for. He began to talk, fast and without pause, launching into an explanation of himself. His background was of sound New England stock. There had never been a serious illness. His schooling was normal and ordinary, through grade and high school, but curtailed in the second year at Brown University. Throughout, there had been the usual vagaries of science-fiction, ranging from Burroughs into Wells and thence to Stapledon, Bradbury, Lovecraft and C.A. Smith.

It seemed a rather odd progression to me and I queried him, "Heinlein? Van Vogt?"

He seemed perturbed at this. No, he pointed out. His predilection in these fields had always leaned to the sheer fantasy and the outré. From his earliest youth he had seemed possessed—even *harried*—by a preternatural perception on the very verge of fulfillment.

Thus in recent years he had become a recognized figure in the field of dimensional hypothesis; but it was recognition with a taint because he called himself a mystic as well. His treatises on the probability of other worlds, dimensional worlds, contained evidence of tangential mystic thought, but so plausible were his theories that few contemporaries dared dispute them. Consequently they ignored them!

"Fire," he said. "And storm," he echoed. "Storm reacts inside me like a catalyst! Can you understand that, Dr. Sherman? It harries my thoughts and pursues my mind until I possess a spirit of—of—" He floundered for words. "There's a feeling I'm about to *accomplish* incredible things, and yet I remain helpless on the threshold. I tell you it becomes sentient! I am permitted to *hear* things, as if—as if each of my atoms were attuned to another dimension!"

"You say—permitted?"

He nodded, staring fixedly into the fire.

"All right," I said, and I observed him carefully. "Would you care to tell me about the things you hear."

ONCE MORE the trembling came, together with that look of despair and helpless longing.

"Music! And it's a violin, always. But so different, so unutterably beautiful that I know it can't be of this world. And just as storm causes me to hear, so does fire cause me to see—as if flame were the gateway, a tangent into other planes..." There was pleading in his voice. "And might it not be? Hasn't fire the power to transmute a block of wood into a different state of being—heat and energy, a higher vibration, the vibration that's the basis of all things? Lately I've felt myself so near, I was almost able to—to—"

"To make the transition," I nodded. I hadn't the heart to tell him this was common practice among certain adepts and laymen too, while in the grip of religious or emotional fervor. "Go on, Maxton. What are the things you...see?"

"I'm not sure. Except that it's always the same scene! Another world, vague distances—a grassy vista reaching away, with trees bordering in the background—strange looking trees beneath a yellow sky. No movement, no sight of any living thing, but across this place comes the sound of the violin! It seems nearer each time, yet I have the feeling that *I'm approaching the music* rather than it approaching me. Then—there comes an unbearable longing, and I know that one of these days—"

Frantically, he seized my arm. "Tell me, tell me! I must be mad. Isn't it true? Or could it be that I'm constituted unlike other people, that my eyes and ears actually *see and hear vibrations* out of our plane. I must know! Is it all of my mind, or do I really have that power?"

I could not answer the poor fellow's questions! He had presented himself so convincingly that I found myself caught up in it, gripped by a new and staggering concept—the idea that those whom we call mad, particularly those who *see and hear* things when there is naught to see and hear, might actually have a different mechanism attuned to vibrations beyond the temporal—

That Joan of Arc for example—and there were innumerable others—who saw visions and heard voices, *might have actually been in contact with another existing plane—*

That some percentage, at least, of those poor unfortunates in our institutions...?

No! I caught myself up just in time. Beyond any doubt, there was in Maxton's fantasy the definite aspect of subliminal resentment (witness the disregard of his theories and writings by his contemporaries in the field) but what was far more interesting to me, *subliminal stimulus* as well! Could it be that such a brilliant thinker as Maxton was a victim of his own convictions, to the extent that he induced these illusions by way of "proving" his postulates about other dimensional worlds?

"You've mentioned this as a recurring thing," I said. "Tell me, when did it all begin?"

"Over a year ago. There was only a hint of it then, but it becomes stronger each time."

"Both visually and audibly?"

He nodded.

"And this...other-worldly violin. You say it's always the same instrument? How do you know it's the same?"

"Because it's still the same melody. Didn't I explain? An initial melody that hasn't ended yet... I've heard it half a dozen times, there's always a series of progressive chords—weaving a slow pattern—" He paced the room, and there was eagerness now. "I have a theory about it. This other dimension impinges on ours, but it has a rate of vibration infinitely faster. So that a simple melody to a person of that world, say the violin-player herself, *wound encompass a year of time as we know it!* I feel it's coming to a close, that melody."

"And then? What do you feel will happen?"

"I don't know!" He paused abruptly, turned to face me and tried to smile. "But it's different than a year ago. I've felt it each time. Not so much fear as—an excitement, a yearning! There's something to come, something vast, and I know that melody is only a prelude...

I knocked the ash from my pipe and slowly refilled it. The man was a paradox! In his narration he had vacillated from fear to distress to harassment, then in doubt, and from there to a subdued sort of eagerness that bordered on expectancy. Talking it out with me had brought about the transition, but somehow I could not believe this had been his intent at all.

We left it there. Professionally my approach had been less than semi-analytic, my curiosity far removed from the insatiable; but this casual attitude did not seem to bother Maxton as it does most, who dangle their "gift" of neurotic functioning in front of the analyst wanting some assurance that the sacrifice will be worth while. Maxton was perfectly composed and certainly rational when he left me that night—but I can't say as much for my own state of mind.

Almost, it was as if our roles had been reversed. The usual answers would not apply. Wasn't Maxton's fantasy merely that—a fantasy—devious to be sure but nevertheless a projected wish fulfillment? Fixation made real and visual and audible due to stress of study and over-work? The subliminal stimulus now manifest as a self-assertive impulse?

No! I could not accept it. Now it was *I* who felt uneasy and disturbed, dissatisfied in a way I had never experienced.

And contributing to this was a factor I had to pin-point! There was something Maxton had said—a thing—a mere mention that escaped me in passing, but I knew it was important now. And like a peck in a drink that bobs and eludes, it eluded me now.

Gradually I relaxed, took my mind away, and as so often happens it popped at once to the surface. I remembered!

Something he had said, just a little thing—*a single word merely, but now it loomed large with implication!*

DR. SHERMAN paused in his telling. Not for so mundane a reason as dramatic effect. His gaze was beyond me, not in present time and space, and he was obviously unaware that he had a visitor.

I glanced at his hands. They were clenched until the knuckles showed white. I waited, and slowly he relaxed, leaning back in his chair as the words came again.

Philip Maxton! I saw him but twice after that. It was some five weeks later that I attended a forum on "Therapy and the Metaphysical Impact," or some such nonsensical thing—the woods are full of these pseudo-discussion groups who sound and expound. I told myself I was interested, but I suppose I attended solely in the hope Maxton would be there. One of the sub-topics was "Vibration and the Structural Dimensions."

Of course Maxton was there. He greeted me in not too pleased a manner, and for the rest of the evening managed to avoid me. His own exposition on the sub-topic was interesting enough but not new, in fact was a summation of his earliest themes, and nowhere did he touch upon the topic he had broached to me. Not until the close of the session did I manage to get him aside.

"Maxton! You may consider this unprofessional as hell—I do myself—but I've got to ask you. Has it happened again? Please believe me, I've got to know!"

He seemed reluctant to talk about it; and I knew at once that something *had* happened; it was obvious he had experienced his phenomenon again. (Note that I was no longer thinking of it as a noumenal!)

"During our last talk," I pursued, "you mentioned a thing I haven't been able to forget. You said there was no sight of any living thing in this other dimension, but then you remarked about the violin-player *herself!*" I paused, watching him. *"Why did you signify the feminine?"*

"What? But I didn't say that! I couldn't—"

"Maxton. You did say it, I assure you."

He stared at me, eyes wide with genuine shock. "But that means I must have known...heaven help me, even then! Even before—"

I spoke very carefully. "Of course. From the very beginning you knew. And since then, you *have* seen her. Isn't that it? Now you are sure."

"Seen her? Yes—how can I ever forget! The barest glimpse only, but I *am* sure! I begin to see the purpose now, the reason for the melody. She needs me, she wants me, just as I—"

His voice was almost a sob. Desire was there, and longing was there, the desire and longing of a man who has seen a vision and finds it suddenly attainable. Then Maxton caught himself sharply; there was a change across his face, a guarded caution as he looked at me, as if he feared that somehow I might invade his private domain!

I placed a hand upon his shoulder, and the trembling of his body seemed to quiet.

"Philip," I said softly. "First of all you must understand that my interest in this thing is purely clinical. You do know that?" He nodded. "So, it will happen again. And perhaps again. And when those times come, we'll disuse it very thoroughly; no doubt you'll have much more to tell. Agreed?"

Again he nodded, but I'm not at all sure that he heard. It was apparent that time for him had a quite separate and personal connotation.

But I knew I would see Philip Maxton again, and I did...for the last time.

IT WAS a month later when he came again to my home. He was a changed man, gaunt and hollow-cheeked with a terrible tiredness about him. But the real difference was in his eyes! Again a paradox. A brilliance was there, a consuming eagerness, nothing now of distress.

It was quite apparent that he looked to me for neither solution nor solace...but why had he come?

It was again a night of storm. It had been building up all day along the coast. I could hear the rush of wind around the Heights and I pictured the waves below, kicking across the bay in mad turmoil against the cliffs. Yes, I could almost see it— and before Maxton was through with me that night I was to see and feel it too!

He talked, now, with an unleash of feeling as if he knew there was little time and he was compelled to let me know.

"Remember, Dr. Sherman. You must promise to remember! Whatever happens, my theories of the dimensions are correct. I shall prove them tonight. I've been close, so close, but most important of all *I have seen her!*"

I cannot say that then, or at any time, I comprehended one-tenth of what was going on in Maxton's mind or the depth of emotion that stirred him. His theme was the same, but now there was something else; almost, it was as if his mind were hung suspended and I caught its quivering.

"...and she's aware that I listen! Do you remember what I told you about the music? My feeling that I'm approaching it rather than it approaching me? Well, it's true, I know that now, and I feel the melody's coming to a close." He was staring into the fire with an intensity that alarmed me. I started to go to him, but he continued:

"Pre-destination. Do you believe in that? The direct pattern of occurrence in our lives? It's more than a phrase of the mystics! I'm convinced that my entire life, all the course of my studies have been directed toward the moment when I might penetrate the barrier and reach *her...*"

Heaven help me, but I found myself caught up by his convictions, the utter loneliness and longing in Maxton's voice! Part of his spell was on me, something of storm and fire and his terrible desire. His voice went on. It must have been minutes. Then abruptly, I caught the sudden sharp tremor that engulfed him.

I might have stopped it! I might have contained him! But it was too late now, for I felt it too...something there in the room with the two of us, a thing illogical and nameless and yet palpable as the scent of fear.

It was *silence* I was aware of, and yet it was a sound that brought me back. A tiny sound as if a log in the fireplace had snapped. I glimpsed Maxton, dimly, but there was a difference now; for the merest instant a haze touched the room and a flame leaped once.

Cold dread dragged at my spine. I couldn't move, and my eyes seemed—

WHAT I seemed to see behind the flame was a great rolling vista of another world with strange grass, lurid-hued, leaping waist high. And then there was no mistaking it. *I saw her.*

With that glimpse, my heart lurched into my throat with terrible longing, and I knew something of what Maxton meant.

She stepped very delicately across the terrain as if not wishing to break the spell. Her face was bowed low across a stringed instrument, upon which she played with a sweeping and heartfelt effort. She was shapely, she was desirable, but more than anything else it was the sound of the music that held me.

Compelling, Maxton had said? It was more! All time seemed to stop. Certainly my heart had stopped. I stood transfixed, as her arm swept across the strings in a final prolonged crescendo that reached and grasped and tugged.

It was then that fear rose to my throat, the sort of fear one experiences when entering a nightmare-dream where evil lurks.

I remember staggering back. I glimpsed Maxton through a glaucous haze and I thought I heard his voice. The music was reaching the end, on a low sustained chord. Beside the maiden, the tall grass rustled in an unfelt breeze. Something—a great furry shape, red jowled, with strange disjointed limbs—rose up from the grass as if impatiently awaiting the moment; apparently it was some pet of hers.

And still she played, drawing out that final strain, swaying a little forward as she peered...

It was then that I saw her face.

It was faintly furred and aquiline, her eyes red and purposeful beneath evilly arched brows, nostrils thin and distended with devilish satisfaction at a deed well done. Lips cruel in a thin slash, but quirked at the corners as if ready to burst into a chortle of glee. A demoniac face, a female face out of hell!

But that was not the real horror. The horror was when Maxton screamed.

I saw him then, or part of him...seemingly *behind* the flames, being drawn and diminished by the last strains of that devil's violin. A horrible transformation was taking place. I saw his body become furry, then slowly alien—shapeless—as his limbs disappeared into vague wavering appendages. There seemed to be three figures now: still the girl, and her beast, and something half hidden, something that was partly Philip Maxton.

It was his eyes I saw, his eyes to the last. Twice more he screamed and each time it sounded different; then something, thick and guttural and not quite human, certainly not a scream.

It was *then* there came the singing snap of the string beneath her hands, jarring my senses. She looked with quick alarm at the broken instrument, then at a spot in my direction. Apparently she saw Maxton, for she leered and seemed vastly pleased.

She reached down and touched her pet, that shapeless furry beast. Her lips moved, addressing it, and I'm sure I heard the words thin and muted:

"There! You see, it did work, and we have another. A companion! You need never be lonely any more..."

They turned, the two of them, and walked away into the lurid grass. I thought I saw another similarly tentacled beast slink along behind...hesitant...frightened and a little bewildered. But I could not be sure. A log in the fireplace snapped, a flame gushed out and the scene fast faded away.

SHERMAN'S story was finished. For a long while he sat hunched forward, oblivious, staring at the floor as if still caught in the spell. As for me—there were no words I could say. I had come for the story, and I had it.

Dumbly I rose and crossed the room. His window faced upon the expanse of lawn and shrubbery that flanked the huge building. Bright sunlight bathed the grounds, and I saw them down there—the others. They strolled harmlessly, mostly by themselves, or just sat on the benches enjoying the sun. Vacant but content.

My face twisting with concern, I came away from the window. "Doctor Sherman..."

He didn't hear, he seemed quite unaware of my presence. Then, from just inside the doorway someone called to me. The attendant—Roberts, I think he said his name was. I realized he must have been waiting near by all the while.

I hurried to him. "Is he—will he be all right?"

"Quite all right," Roberts assured me.

"Perhaps I shouldn't have—"

"No, quite the contrary. We're happy you came! His symptoms are not distressing, but there are inhibitory factors;

occasionally he needs such an assertive outflow. Makes him more amenable to treatment."

"Will he ever—you know—be the same again?"

Roberts considered it. "Perhaps, in time. Perhaps never. This is an absolutely unprecedented case."

I took a last look about the room. It was small but comfortably furnished. My gaze stopped at a row of volumes. "He still has his books..."

"Oh, yes. Sherman is very special here."

I stepped over to the books, and Roberts came quickly beside me. "Don't touch them! Ordinarily he's quite rational, but he becomes frantic if anyone—"

So I merely looked. They were thin books, obviously the sort that are privately printed, but the titles were impressive. *Vibration and the Structural Dimensions,* by Philip Maxton. *Patterns of Flux: An Observation,* by Philip Maxton. There were a dozen others in similar vein, all by Maxton.

Something struck me now, a sudden grotesque thought. I gasped, but couldn't bring myself to voice it. "I don't understand," I said. "His story seemed so real, but there's still something I can't quite...all this business about Philip Maxton..."

Roberts looked at me, not smiling. "I think you understand, all right. Certainly you don't suppose the thing happened? Or that there ever was a Philip Maxton? These are all Sherman's works. He wrote the stuff himself."

I nodded, and now I was aware that Doctor Sherman had raised his head. He was watching us closely. Perhaps he had heard the word "Maxton."

Something triggered him. Rising, he walked over and extended a hand to me. It was warm and firm and friendly. "You mustn't go yet," he said. "Don't you remember? There is something I promised to show you. The golden string. The string from the violin."

He seemed quite rational again as he stepped to a table, opened the drawer and took out a tiny lacquered box. He reached into the box and carefully brought up his hand, finger and thumb extended; his eyes were needle bright, his mien exultant. Here was irrefutable proof!

I peered and my breath caught in my throat. For a moment I actually saw it, I was positive, the thin golden strand twisting like a thing alive beneath his fingers.

Almost...and then I peered again and knew.

There was no string in his fingers. There was nothing there at all. Nothing...

THE END

YES, BURT, THERE IS A SANTA CLAUS

by Gregory Luce
Copyright 2013 by Gregory J. Luce

Santa was all for giving lumps of coal to little kids who weren't good all year…but he had a quite different approach for adults!

There weren't too many people around town that didn't like kids. Burt Gibbs was one, though. He hated them. Keep in mind, we're not talking about a mild or even strong dislike, this guy *really* hated kids. Their whiny voices made him cringe with annoyance, like the feeling you get when long fingernails are dragged across a classroom chalkboard. Most of the kids in Burt's neighborhood knew him by reputation and cautiously steered clear of his ramshackle cottage, but ignorant little tykes who ventured in from the outside were usually caught by surprise. Grade school girls who came around selling Girl Scout cookies were guaranteed to get a door slammed in their startled faces. Little boys were treated no differently—Burt was very democratic about that kind of thing—except with them he usually threw in a choice four-letter word or two as he told them to get the hell off his doorstep. Heaven help the youngster who tried to cut through his lawn, Burt's enraged curses usually echoed all the way around the block.

That's why the whole neighborhood choked with disbelief when he was seen at the local shopping mall on Christmas Eve, playing none other than the great bearded one himself, Santa Claus. That's right—Santa Claus, Kris Kringle, Old Saint Nick, the greatest kid lover in the history of the world. It was like somebody's idea of a sick joke.

On the other hand, the people at the mall thought Burt was great, a real godsend. Their other Santa—the one who'd been working since the day after Thanksgiving—had come down with a particularly nasty case of the stomach flu that had sent him into an all-night jam-session with his toilet bowl. So there they were, Christmas Eve morning with no Santa Claus for the hundreds of last minute kiddies that would come traipsing through the mall entrance.

Then Burt walked in, not that he wanted the job, mind you, but he just happened to be in the right place at the wrong time. He'd been working at the mall as a custodian for over three years, and at 6'4" and 290 pounds, he was perfect for the role of Santa—from a physical standpoint, anyway. When the other Santa called in sick at eight-thirty that morning, the mall manager, Mr. Jenkins, yanked Burt into his office and literally begged him to fill in for their ailing superstar. After all, it was only for a few hours and the mall was scheduled to close early that day, at 6:00 p.m. Burt protested vehemently, but Jenkins promised him double time-and-a-half, plus Super Bowl Sunday off. Burt relented.

So there he was, dressed to the tee like the old toy maker himself, sitting in that uncomfortable wooden throne in "Santa's Square," waiting for the forthcoming onslaught of nose-mining rug rats. The mall doors opened. The rush was on.

Jenkins was standing alongside Burt's ornamental throne when the first people started trickling into the mall.

"Just remember all the basics," Jenkins said.

"Yeah, sure," Burt replied.

"Smile and say hello, then ask their name and age."

"I remember, I remember."

"Ask them if they've been good kids all year."

"Now that's a joke—"

"Ask them what all they want from Santa."

"As if they won't be shovin' that down my throat anyway."

"And be sure to give every child a candy cane."

"Will ya just relax. I can handle these little creeps. Trust me." Burt was thinking other things. *Yeah, I'll break their little necks.* His teeth were already grinding and he hadn't even had a toddler on his lap, yet.

"Remember, Tina will be taking all the Polaroids, so look happy and smile big," Jenkins said, putting his hand on the 17-

year-old girl's shoulder. "I'll be back in a few minutes to see how you're both doing."

As Jenkins left, Tina—who was scantily clad in a skimpy elf's costume—tossed a broad, sickeningly sweet smile in Burt's direction. "Don't worry, this is gonna be fun for *both* of us. Most of these little kids are *so* cute."

Burt thought he was going to throw up. Super Bowl or no Super Bowl, this just wasn't worth it. But it was too late, there was no escape, the first rug rats were approaching.

"Stinkin' little crumbcrushers," he muttered to himself.

Burt's first customers stood at the head of a waiting line that formed quickly. A five-year-old girl and her mother stepped forward. He let out a deep sigh, then said it: "Hi there little kid, what's your name?"

As the first couple of hours dragged by, Burt managed to get through them somehow without embarrassing the mall too badly, or without making it too obvious to the little darlings sitting in his lap that he was the furthest thing from Santa Claus since Ebenezer Scrooge.

For Burt, though, it was pure hell. By 12:30 over a hundred tykes had sat on his lap: eight had cried, two had farted, and nine—frozen with awe at Santa's presence—had refused to say anything. Burt kept eyeing the large clock hanging from the mall rafters in longing anticipation of lunch.

At a few minutes to one, Jenkins strolled over to see how the mall's new Santa was doing. There was a four-year-old girl babbling away on Burt's lap. Jenkins leaned over the retaining fence and whispered into Tina's ear, "Well, how's he doing?"

Tina winced slightly, then whispered back, "He's doing...okay...I guess. He's kinda gruff. I don't think he likes kids too much."

"Has he pissed anybody off yet?"

"Uhhh...there've been a few people that have looked at him kinda funny, but nobody's said anything so far. One lady laughed at him." She chuckled softly. "He doesn't know what to say...you know...especially when some of the smaller kids are just sitting there not saying anything either. They just...kind of stare at each other." She paused and laughed quietly again.

Jenkins rolled his eyes and shook his head. They both glanced at Burt. The four-year-old was still yapping away. Snot was trickling out of her left nostril. Burt cringed. Tina started giggling uncontrollably as a drop of it dripped on Burt's leg; even Jenkins almost broke out laughing.

The mall manager seemed to sense his replacement Santa was on the edge of cracking, so he stepped around the retaining fence and over to the people in line.

"Folks, Santa's going on break in a couple of minutes," Jenkins announced. "He's got eight hungry reindeer that need feeding so he'll be gone for a short while, but he'll be back in about thirty minutes...right around 1:30." He turned toward Burt. The four-year-old was just climbing off his knee.

"Ready, Santa?"

"This'll cost you the next *ten* Super Bowl Sundays."

With Jenkins and Tina flanking him, Burt walked down the exit isle and back toward the mall's main office and lunch room. His workday in hell was nearly half over.

* * *

Seven-year-old Jody McCallister was waiting for his mom to pick him up from Hillcrest Daycare Center. He was normally there from three to five every afternoon, but this week—his second grade class being out for Christmas break—it had been an all-day affair, everyday.

Christmas Eve was a day of true excitement for Jody. Mom was going to pick him up after work, and the pair of them would head straight to the mall for their annual visit with Santa Claus.

Jody could hardly wait. Santa was *the* man as far as he was concerned—the greatest super hero of all time. He'd scrawled out a list of presents on a sheet of tablet paper and was going to make sure the great bearded one knew about every one of them.

He'd also made his own gift for Santa, a small reindeer cut out of brown paper.

Later in the evening, Grandma and Grandpa would be over. If Jody pleaded hard enough, there was a chance they'd lean on Mom and convince her to let him rip into one of his presents before Christmas morning. Grandma and Grandpa were great about stuff like that. Then, at bedtime, his stocking would be hung in glorious anticipation of the annual visit by Santa and his eight flying reindeer. It was going to be an evening filled with titillating anticipation.

Jody and his mom lived in a small, upper-story two-bedroom apartment. Jody didn't mind too much, but his mother had seemed dispirited and withdrawn much of the time since they'd moved there two years ago. Jody had thought a lot about that. He figured things would get better when Dad got back. That would help Mom out a lot. Jody hadn't seen him since he was five, but he was coming back any day now. Mom kept saying so. When Dad came home it would fix everything.

At a few minutes past five, Jody heard a familiar voice. "Hey, kiddo, how's it going?"

He looked up and saw his mother walking briskly into the room.

"Mom!" he cried, running to her. They exchanged a warm hug amidst the various toys that littered the playroom floor.

"Come on, buddy," she said as he wriggled free of her arms. "We've got to get downtown and see Santa. The mall closes in less than an hour."

Helen McCallister signed the check-out sheet while Jody grabbed his jacket and paper reindeer. The two of them then hurried to the idling car outside. The mall, and Santa, were just a few minutes away.

* * *

When lunch break was over, Jenkins practically had to put a gun to Burt's head to get him back out on the mall floor. He knew Gibbs wasn't the best man for the job, but it was far too late to find another substitute Santa.

"I'm not goin' back out there…period!" Burt told him bluntly. He started changing back into his street duds, but Jenkins—in a somewhat diplomatic, typical mall manager fashion—reminded his deserting toy-maker of the importance of continued employment.

"This is below the belt…kickin' a man when he's down…it's…it's…gawd-damn blackmail, that's what it is!" Burt exclaimed in an irritated tone.

When Santa got back to his throne he found a line of over 30 gawking youngsters waiting for him. It was too much. He needed a way out. A warped, twisted thought came into Burt's mind…

Suicide.

That was it; he could see the headlines now: SANTA CLAUS BLOWS BRAINS OUT INSIDE LOCAL MALL— what a story!

A brief smattering of applause sounded as Burt settled back into Santa's chair. He looked at the waiting line contemptuously. If they only knew what he was really thinking. He was ready to club the first kid that got out of line. His tongue was primed, like a hair trigger, waiting to fire a fusillade of world-class obscenities at the first snot-nosed kid that provoked him. It was only with the greatest of restraint—and the knowledge that Jenkins was standing a few feet to his right—that Burt was able to rise to the occasion and continue on.

Much to Jenkins' relief, things went fairly smooth for the next few hours. Even Burt was surprised. The crowds had thinned out by mid-afternoon, and Tina—at Jenkins' request— was doing most of the talking.

Shortly after five, Burt began to see the light at the end of tunnel. There hadn't been a kid in line for over five minutes, and people were beginning to file out of the mall. In less than an hour, he'd be free. What a relief. He glanced up—it was almost 5:30. Only a little while longer, then it was *Adios Santa!*

Just then, a man with a two-and-a-half-year-old in tow walked into Santa's Square.

"Hi there, little man. Come to see Santa Claus?" Tina asked. Her sickeningly sweet countenance hadn't diminished all day.

"This is Billy's first visit to Santa," replied the father.

Little Billy stood staring at Burt with his index finger stuck in his mouth.

"How'd you like to tell Santa about all those toys you want for Christmas?" Tina coaxed him.

The boy shook his head.

"Come on, Billy," said the father. "Let's go say hello." He lifted the child up and sat him on Burt's knee.

"Hey there, Billy. How's it goin'?" Santa asked.

Billy shook his head, his index finger still stuck in his mouth.

"Can ya tell me how old you are?"

Billy shook his head again.

"What all do ya want for Christmas?"

Billy kept on shaking his head.

"Do ya understand anything I'm sayin' to ya?"

Another shake.

Tina and Billy's father started to laugh, and for a moment, even Burt Gibbs found the situation mildly amusing. Maybe he was getting used to it, or maybe this little house ape *was* kind of cute.

Billy started to fidget on Santa's knee.

"Well, I'll tell you what, Billy," Burt said, reaching into his pocket for a candy cane. "You seem like a pretty good kid, and Santa's gonna be sure to—" he stopped short. A warm, wet feeling was extending down his right leg. He lifted Billy up and looked at his trousers.

"Gahhhhhhh!"

Billy had peed on Santa Claus.

Burt sat there for a moment, holding the child in mid-air. Urine was still dripping from Billy's pants onto Santa's leg. He'd been duped. This little ankle biter was no different than the rest of them.

Tina's eyes went wide and her mouth dropped open. She started to laugh.

"Uh-oh," said Billy's father. "Looks like a little accident."

"Somebody get this soggy little kid away from me!" Burt was ready to explode. He stood up and sat Billy on the floor. His right leg was soaked and he could feel warm urine running down his boot.

"I am *so* sorry about this." Billy's father said, obviously embarrassed. "We've been potty-training him for the last couple of months and—"

"I don't care! Do ya hear me? *I...don't...care!*" Burt looked daggers at Tina, who was failing miserably at controlling her laughter.

"I'm outa here. I'm gone. I'm history!" Burt proclaimed in an agitated voice.

Billy sat on the floor, still shaking his head.

Burt threw the candy cane on the floor and stomped down the exit isle.

"Well, excuse us all to hell," Billy's father called out to the retreating Santa.

Tina's expression turned apologetic. "I'm really sorry. He's had a pretty tough day." Then she started giggling again.

At the moment Burt Gibbs was clomping into the nearby men's room, another young boy and his mother were coming up Santa's walkway.

"Is Santa Claus still here?" Helen McCallister asked the young girl in elf's costume.

"I'm afraid not," answered Tina. "There was a little accident here a couple of minutes ago and I don't think he'll be back."

"Mom!" A sound of sudden disappointment was in Jody's voice.

Helen looked pleadingly at Tina. "The ad in the paper said he'd be here 'til the mall closed. What happened, anyway?"

Tina tried to explain what had happened without blowing Santa's real identity in front of Jody.

"You're positive he's not coming back?" asked Helen.

"I—really don't think so."

"Mom! He's gotta come back…I got my list!" Jody appealed in a desperate voice.

Tina looked at the boy. "I'm awfully sorry. I just don't think—"

"You don't understand. I *have* to give him my list of presents."

"I'll tell you what, I'm going to see Santa in the manager's office in a few minutes and I'll be sure to give him your list…okay?"

"You can do that for us?" Helen asked.

Tina nodded. "Oh, sure. I'll stick it right in front of his nose if I have to."

Jody felt a certain amount of relief as he handed Tina the list, but great disappointment remained. He wanted to *see* Santa, not just pass off his list to some poor messenger girl.

"Here's a candy cane for you, and I promise to make sure Santa sees your list." Tina placed the candy in Jody's hand.

"Well…what do you say, Jody?" his mother asked.

The boy looked down at his shoelaces, slumping dejectedly. "Thank you," he said in a glum tone.

As Jody and his mother passed out of Santa's Square, feelings of disappointment grew stronger inside the youngster's mind. It was the worst kind of letdown for a kid at Christmas time. Seeing Santa had meant a great deal to Jody, but now it would be another year and another Christmas before he could see him again. In Jody's mind it was a total rip-off.

As Helen and Jody made their way toward the mall exit, suddenly another feeling came over the seven-year-old.

"Mom."

"Yeah, hon."

"I gotta go to the bathroom."

Helen led her son over to the tile-covered entryway of the men's restroom.

"I'm going to use the ladies room while you're inside. If you come out before I do, just wait for me…okay?"

Jody nodded his head.

Meanwhile, inside the men's room, Burt Gibbs had pulled off his right boot.

The bladder size of most two-and-a-half-year-olds was quite small, but little Billy had been an exception. Burt's lower pant leg and sock were soaked. He'd really hit the mother lode with this kid. He pulled off the yellow-stained sock and held it over a toilet bowl, then wrung it out.

As he stood watching the drops of urine fall into the toilet, a wave of kid-kicking ferocity came over him. He wanted to slam a little hand in a car door. Maybe that would make him feel better.

Then the restroom door opened.

Jody McCallister walked in and was stunned by what he saw. There was Santa Claus himself, standing in front of a toilet wearing one boot and holding a wet sock in his hands.

Jody's eyes lit up. "Hi, Santa!"

Burt grimaced at the sound of the voice. He looked over his shoulder and saw the seven-year-old standing behind him.

"Oh, gawd…"

He picked up his boot, threw the wet sock into it, and headed for the restroom door.

As Burt walked past, Jody glanced down at the brown paper reindeer he was still holding. He hadn't left it with Tina. He was going to save it for tonight when Santa came. He'd planned on leaving it—along with a note—next to his stocking. But everything was changed now. Here was Santa—in person! The day was saved.

"Santa, wait!"

Burt stopped, then slowly turned. "What do ya want, kid?" There was an edge to his voice.

Jody was taken aback by Santa's irritated tone, and his eyes, they looked *mean.* Something was wrong. Jody didn't understand; he almost froze, but managed to open his mouth.

"I—I made this for you in daycare today."

"What is it?"

"See…it's a…a reindeer." Jody timidly stepped over and placed the brown paper cutout in Santa's free hand.

At that moment, an uncontrollable desire for revenge swept through Burt Gibbs' brain. He hated kids. He'd always hated kids. They'd put him through hell today, and now they were going to pay for it. He sat his boot down on the floor.

"Here, kid. Here's something for you, too." His hands went into a series of frantic tearing motions. Then he stretched them out over the boy's head.

Jody's eyebrows raised and he let out a gasp.

"Have some confetti." Burt opened his hands and pieces of brown paper went fluttering to the floor.

Jody couldn't believe what he was seeing. Tears started to well up in his eyes.

Then Burt did the unthinkable. He leaned over into the face of the seven-year-old—*and pulled down his beard!*

"There *ain't* no Santy Claus, kid…get it! Now quit buggin' me!" The beard snapped back over his face. Burt grabbed the boot and marched out the door. Santa was gone.

Jody stood there and swallowed hard. His facial muscles constricted and his eyes released a sudden flash flood of tears as he started to cry. It was the kind of sobbing that really tears a heart out. He stood there weeping, paralyzed with hurt.

After a minute or two, a soft knock sounded at the door. "Jody? Are you in there?"

Helen McCallister heard the crying and stuck her head inside. Standing in the middle of the men's room was her seven-year-old son, sobbing under his breath, tears of betrayal streaming down his cheeks. She hurried across the room to him.

"Honey…what happened?"

"Mom, Santa yelled at me!" he cried to her.

"What?"

"He pulled off his beard. He—he said I was bothering him and that there wasn't—there wasn't really any Santa Claus." Jody's words were almost garbled from his sobbing. "He ripped up my reindeer, too." His finger pointed to the torn pieces of brown paper that lay on the cold floor.

Helen looked down at the remnants; her face flushed with sudden anger.

"A man dressed like Santa Claus was in here?"

Jody nodded.

"And he said all those things to you?"

Another nod.

"And he ripped up your reindeer?" Her voice was seething.

Jody began to sob again as he nodded one more time.

Helen's anger was turning to rage. She wasn't exactly sure what had happened, but she was going to find out—*now*. She reached for her son's hand.

"Honey, come with me."

They marched out of the men's room, Helen practically dragging Jody behind her. There was a look of murder in her eyes. Someone had done this horrible thing to her boy, and there was going to be hell to pay.

They walked up to the information booth near the mall entrance.

"Can you tell me where I can find the mall manager?"

The lady in the booth had been smiling, but it quickly faded from her face. "I'm not sure if he's still here. It's almost six o'clock." She looked at Jody's reddened eyes. "What happened to your boy?"

Helen pointed toward the restroom. "Some idiot dressed up like Santa—"

At that instant, everything went dark. The entire mall was thrown into blackness. A mass cry of surprise rose up from the hundreds of shoppers that were still trickling off the mall floor. The power had obviously gone out.

Burt Gibbs, having changed back into his civvies in Jenkins' office, was making a hasty getaway out the mall's side exit when the blackout occurred. As he stepped outside he realized it wasn't just the mall, nearly half the city was black. Everything on the east side of Riverside Avenue had suddenly been plunged into darkness. Burt figured one of Pacific Power's main transformers must have blown sky high.

"What the hell? Will ya lookit this," he muttered to himself, gazing out into the darkness.

He started trudging across the parking lot toward the Bear Creek bike path, which was just on the other side of the mall's perimeter roadway. Burt had always walked to work. It was just a ten-minute trek down the bike path and across Hawthorne Park to home, but he'd never traversed it in such dim gloominess.

Inside the mall, the McCallisters waited for the lights to come back on, but after a couple of minutes they gave up and started stumbling through the darkness. They followed the herd of exiting shoppers that was grabbling its way toward the exits. Helen was fuming as she guided her weepy son through the dimness of the huge shopping center. The exit was close, though, and they made their way outside a few moments later.

After finding their car, Helen and Jody piled in the front seat and sped off toward their apartment on the west side of town. Helen's mind continued to seethe from the verbal and mental abuse that the psycho-Santa from the mall had dished out on her son. When she found out who the insensitive jerk was behind the phony Santa beard, he was going to pay dearly. Her son's Christmas was probably ruined; the meager presents she'd been able to afford would probably do little to offset the shattering of his reverent belief in Old Saint Nick.

After they pulled into the apartment parking lot, Helen sat in the car and did her best to convince Jody that the man from the men's room was some kind of an imposter. The real Santa Claus was alive and well and coming tonight. She looked into his eyes—he wasn't buying it. A feeling of resignation came over her. The idiot from the mall had blown it for her son; Christmas would never be the same for Jody again. Tears now came to her eyes, too.

"Come on, honey. Let's go inside."

The two of them climbed out of the vehicle and made their way up the apartment stairs.

Over on the Bear Creek bike path, Burt Gibbs was groping along in the dark, trying to keep on the pathway. The power was still out over most of the city. It was only a little past six o'clock, but any earlier traces of daylight were completely gone now. A full moon would rise later that evening, but the starlight was obscured by a thick blanket of clouds that left the trail in a gloomy darkness. Burt could barely see five feet in front of him.

"Damn this dark. I can't hardly see a friggin' thing," he muttered.

He trudged along at a very slow, tentative gate. The paved pathway followed Bear Creek throughout the length of the city, and for a short stretch it ran along the west side of Hawthorne Park. Burt was only a short distance from the park's entry trail when something sounded from behind.

Bleat!

He stopped and turned around. There was nothing—only the rippling sound of Bear Creek, a few yards away.

He turned back slowly and continued on. Probably some night bird or other critter he thought to himself. Or maybe it was his infantile friend from the mall come seeking revenge. Ha! He'd gotten the best of that grubby little house-ape. Burt started to chuckle in the gloom as he thought of his merciless behavior in the men's room. "Sure scared the crap outta that stupid brat," he muttered to himself, smiling.

Bleat!

There it was again. He turned quickly and squinted hard. His eyes strained, but there was still nothing—just blackness. He paused for a few moments, listening carefully. The rushing sound of Bear Creek seemed to camouflage everything within earshot. Maybe it was his imagination. Maybe the sound of the creek had fooled him. That was it—only the sound of the creek, probably nothing more. He turned and continued on. The park was just up ahead.

Bleat! Bleat!

Burt whirled around.

"Who's there?"

There was no doubt in his mind this time—*something* was out there. Fear rose from the pit of his stomach and swelled through the rest of his body.

"Dammit anyway! Who's out there?"

There was no response.

Burt turned and started to trot. Darkness or no darkness, he was getting the hell out of there. The park was coming up on his left, a quick dash across it, and he'd be home.

Crack!

Burt screamed as he felt something strike his back. The pain was sudden and searing. He stumbled onto the hard surface of the pathway, squirming with terror.

Bleat! Bleat! Bleat!

"Get away from me, you sons a' bitches!" He rose to his feet and broke into a dead run. In the dimness he caught sight of the park entry trail. He galloped up the incline and broke out into the open expanse just over the top.

Then he heard it.

Something from behind was following him into the park. His ears detected barely audible, "swishing" noises—like arms flailing in mid-air. There was also the sound of something softly creaking, like an old wooden ship.

Bleat! Bleat! Crack!

Burt screamed again and fell face forward into the moist turf. Something had slashed across the right side of his face. The flash of searing pain was nearly overpowering. He reached up and felt blood oozing from his face.

"Help me! Somebody!" Burt screamed. If he could only make it to a street. East Main was only another hundred yards or so to his right. Maybe he could flag down a passing car.

He struggled to his feet again and stumbled forward a few yards. A wave of horror overtook his senses as he realized the noises had now changed: they were coming from behind and *above*.

Bleat—Bleat! Crack! Crack!

Burt was hit twice more, and this time it put him down for good. As he lay there screaming in agony, a sudden flash of realization came to him: *he was being whipped!*

The strange swishing and creaking sounds were more pronounced now and they seemed to be circling him from a few yards above.

Burt rose to his knees and looked upward. "Get the hell away from me!"

Then a series of sharp pains gouged his body. He could feel his flesh twisting, his bones buckling. His hands began to quake. As he looked at them, a chill of unthinkable horror shot through his brain.

His hands were beginning to transform!

Burt's screaming pierced the cold December air, but nobody heard. As he knelt there, eyes glued to his hands, he saw his fingers wither and merge into fleshy stumps; then large, bony stubs broke through the outer skin. His hands were no longer hands; they were slowly changing into *hoofs*.

He fell over on his back and convulsed like a fish on a dock. The same, pain-racking metamorphosis was spreading to his feet. Then, tremors of physical change flooded the rest of his body. His clothes ripped and fell onto the grass. Bony projectiles erupted from either side of his temples. His nose and mouth seemed to extend outward and merge together.

Somehow, Burt Gibbs rose up.

"Ye-ahhh!" Crack!

He was struck again. He tried to scream, but the sound his throat emitted was no longer human: *"Bleat! Bleat!"*

"Ye-ahhh!" Crack! Crack!

Burt tried to run again, but could only scurry on all fours. Somehow though, he struggled on. He focused his concentration on keeping moving. He must try to run faster, even if it was on all fours.

"*Ye-ahhh!*"

Burt kept going. His mind had grown dull from the excruciating pain and horror he'd suffered. He no longer knew where he was. But presently the pain seemed to subside. As he ran on, his feeling of fear receded, also. It slowly gave way to something else, something Burt Gibbs was completely unfamiliar with, something he'd never felt before...a swelling sense of purpose and destiny.

"*Ye-ahhh!*" *Crack!*

Burt felt consciousness slipping away from him, but he kept on moving. The harder he ran, the stronger he felt. A sudden feeling of inner peace swept through his soul. There was a goal to his life now, a mission to be fulfilled.

The last thing Burt Gibbs consciously felt was a sense of goodness creeping into his heart.

"*Ye-ahhh!*"

The cold evening air rushed against his face as he ran on and on.

*   *   *

It was 2:00 a.m. Jody McCallister had been fast asleep under his covers for several hours, yet something caused him to stir. A dream-like voice seemed to call through the misty clouds of his dreams and beckon to him. His sleep-filled eyes opened slightly. The sky had cleared, and the light of the full moon shone into his bedroom, giving it a soft, luminescent glow. As he sat up in bed he was startled to see his room filled with a treasure of toys! There were all kinds—big ones, little ones—just about everything he could ever want. His eyes went wide with disbelief.

"Wow!"

He slid to the floor with great excitement and began to examine his newfound possessions, but after a moment, the dream-like voice called to him again. This time it seemed to come from beyond his bedroom window, far off in the distance. As he crept softly across his room, he saw the note that lay on the windowsill. He picked it up and read it.

Dear Jody, Always be good, and always believe. Let these precious gifts help you to keep the wonder of your childhood alive. Love, Santa.

The young boy opened his bedroom window and leaned out. The air was crisp, and a cold December wind rushed past his face, gently nibbling his nose and ears. In the distance, wispy, white clouds sailed across the radiant face of the moon. The child's innocence of spirit seemed to glow in the soft, lunar light. He then beheld a magical scene few children have ever witnessed. Crossing in front of the moon, filling the boy with wonder and ecstasy, was the astonishing sight of Santa Claus and his *nine* reindeer!

Out of the nighttime sky the boy heard a distant voice, and it called to him: *"Merry Christmas to all, and to all a good night!"*

THE END

ALL OF YOU

By James McConnell

No woman on Earth could ever love like this!

How well I remember you, my darling. I see you even now as I saw you then, that strange orange evening when your silver steed plunged down to find a haven upon my world of Frth. Even these months hence I can picture in exact detail the full male warmth of your glorious body as it was that hallowed night. I can recall in minuteness the wavy black and silver of your hair, the soothing ruddiness of your complexion and the enticing brownness of your eyes.

Run, run, oh, my darling!

I had been with the other women that first night and was returning to my dwelling by myself when I saw the tongue of flame lash across the sky. For a moment I thought the gods were spitting fire at me. But then the flame melted to earth a short distance away, its amber heat searing the foliage to a charred blue. And through the flame I made out the silver sheen of your carriage.

You will never understand the emotions that caught at me when I realized who and what you might be! When I was young, the Matriarch had mentioned the coming of gods who rode in fiery chariots, but in the intervening years I had lapsed into disbelief. And suddenly, as if to prove the error of my lagging faith, you appeared. Will you ever comprehend the overwhelming sensations I felt that night?

I ran to you then with the speed of a thousand, as you must run tonight.

Faster, my love, faster! Tonight your fear must give you wings!

THE fire had burned a path to your chariot when I reached it, and I ran through the hot ashes heedless of the pain to my naked feet. For I knew that you must be inside, waiting for me to come to you. The door was open, and so I entered.

And you were there, crouched behind some monstrous piece of metal, hoping, perhaps, to shield your glorious body from my sight. But I looked and saw your wonderful stature and knew at once that my heart was lost to you forever. The empathetic organs of my body began to pulsate with devotion. My mind reached out and touched at yours, offering to you the utter devotion of an eternal slave.

What a delicious thing it is to recall the delicate trembling of your beautiful jowls as you looked at me, determining, I am sure, my worth and worthiness. But I had faith. Remember that my darling. I knew that you would not deny me the companionship I so avidly sought.

For a long time—what a horribly delightful time it was for me—you stayed huddled in your corner, immobile save for the scarcely perceptible quivering of your tantalizing body. Until I could stand it no longer and moved forward to caress you. And you opened your eyes widely as if to see me better and raised your hands in the universal sign of acceptance and resignation. And I knew that you were mine!

I reached my long and hopelessly slender arms around the glory of your soft and yielding torso and felt the rapid and elated beating of your heart. And I led you gently from your heavenly steed to the quiet coolness of my love-dwelling.

I AWOKE before you did that bright morning after the night you came to me. For a long time I lay beside you, thrilled by the warmth of your flesh, my eyes closed to the delicious experience. And then, you too awoke and my mind made contact with yours.

"Where am I?"

As you spoke these words your eyes traveled up and down the length of my reclining body. I entered your mind half hesitantly, fearful of what I would find there. For I am still young and ill-formed, running to slenderness instead of to the corpulence that is the universal mark of beauty.

But, oh, my darling, what a great and overwhelming pleasure it was to find that you seemed to approve of what you saw, and in your mind I beheld visions of pleasures which I had before then only dreamed of. Somehow, to you, I seemed beautiful, and I was glad.

And then I felt the tenor of your thinking shift and you repeated, "Where am I?"

I told you with my mind, and then again with my voice. But still you did not understand. And so I drew on the ground a picture of the sun and the other five planets and wrote *FRTH* in large letters by ours, the sixth planet, and made you realize that this was where you were. Then, I pointed to the fifth planet and again at you.

In your supreme cleverness you caught on at once.

"No," you said softly, "I am not from there." You drew on the ground some distance away another sun, surrounded by nine planets, and pointed out the third. "Here's my home."

YOU smiled then and lay back on the couch. Your mind clouded a bit, and although I could follow all your thoughts, many of them seemed strange and incomprehensible.

"Good ole Mother Earth. Home, Sweet Home. I don't even know where it is from here. Lost, that's what I am, lost. Maybe I'll never see New York again, never again eat clam chowder, never watch another baseball game, never again see her."

You began to cry. I reached out to you, taking you into my arms, running my fingers slowly through your hair, sending you comforting and sympathetic thoughts.

"I hated it. I despised Earth—loathed it. And everybody on it," you wept. "Most of all I hated her. Oh, I loved her, but I came to hate her. Can you understand?

"She was beautiful, wonderful, just what I'd always wanted. She was the first pretty girl who ever looked at me twice, and I was 35 years old. So we got married. And that first night—oh, God!"

You looked up at me, your face in tears, your pleasing double chins red from the bending of your neck. I stroked your face gently, soothingly.

"That first night—our honeymoon—when I came to her, she *laughed!* Can you understand that? Laughed! 'You're a fat beast,' she, said. 'Get away from me. I never want to see you again, you obese slob!' I could have killed her!

"She had tricked me, because of my money. I never saw her again, but I hated her with all my heart. And there was another girl, later, who laughed at me too. I couldn't stand it, so I bought the spaceship and just headed out, away from Earth. Nobody wanted me there."

You were still crying. I leaned over and kissed you. If the women of your planet were such fools not to appreciate you, it was not my fault. How badly I wanted you!

You looked up at me and smiled after I kissed you. I entered your mind again and shared contentment with you. For you were thinking of the love we had known the night before, and I was pleased.

Go on, go on! Faster yet! For the spell of love is not yet complete.

IT WAS later that I arose and prepared for the first meal at the day. Succulent fruit I took and threaded them with rich, heavy cream. Nuts from the biggest trees I opened for you, warming their savory meats over the open fire. Fat grubs, rescued from more predatory insects, I basted in their own juices until they turned a golden amber, full of flesh-giving energy.

And all the time I worked, I sang to myself. I was very happy, for it is the purpose of the happy woman to protect the beauty of her chosen male. And as I looked at you, thinking of the food, I knew that you would grow in weight; that you would increase in stature beyond even the fondest dreams of any woman on Frth.

"I...I think I will call you Josephine," you told me as you ate. "And I will be your Napoleon. We'll live here forever in exile. And we'll do nothing all day long but—eat," you said, winking at me and reaching for more fruit and cream. My heart wanted to burst!

"I don't guess I could tell you how much it means to me, your liking me and all that. For the first time in my life, I'm happy. I feel like I really *belong,* if you know what—" You broke off. "Oh, oh. Here comes somebody. Is it all right for me to be here?"

And then it was I saw them, coming down the path towards us—the grandmother and the mother and the elder sisters, six of them in all. But it was the grandmother who spoke to us, as was befitting her station.

"This is the one—the male who came in last night's rain of golden fire?"

I could see her eyes covering you, coveting you.

"Yes, most honored Matriarch. He is one of the god-men from beyond our sun."

"What do they want, Josephine?" you asked, for of course you could not understand their words.

"He is well formed, is he not, my child?" the grandmother said. I could sense even as she spoke these words the horrible fate she had planned for us in her wicked jealousy.

"He is most beautiful, beloved Mother."

"And you feel since you were the one who found him, since it was you who first took him in, that you should have the first and claimant rights to him?" she asked with soft avarice.

"He is mine, most hallowed of women. We love one another, and he is to be the father of my children. The fates have willed it so."

The old woman's voice crashed with thunder: "He is not yours! He belongs to all of us—then to the one who is best qualified to receive him as a husband!"

"Have I done something wrong, Josephine?"

I could not answer you, beloved, for my heart was in my mouth. I knew the trickery that this one, my own parent, was capable of.

The Matriarch was waiting for a sign of opposition so that she could have me destroyed. But I was too clever for that. Even though it meant losing face in your sight for the moment, I offered no resistance.

"He will be taken to the man-compound at once, to be held there until the official beginning of the mating season," she roared, hoping again to provoke me to open hostility. When I made no move, she changed her tactics. "What a wonderful husband he will make," she repeated, again eyeing the splendor of your physique. "How many children he will father for some lucky woman."

I could scarcely stand her taunts, but already, most dear one to my heart, a plan was forming in my mind. You would be mine yet!

"Guards, take him away!" the Old One shouted.

"Josephine, what are they doing? Don't let them take me away from you! I love you, Josephine! Tell them that I'll marry you. Don't let them take me away!"

I felt the confusion in your mind, the lostness that overwhelmed you as my rude sisters led you away from me. And how much I desired to tell you that I was lost too. How much I wanted to tell you to wait patiently until the time was ripe.

But now, my heart's desire, you must not wait, you must not tarry. Oh, there! You've stumbled! Get up, my love! Stand up and run! For death is close behind you!

THAT first night away from you, how my body ached with loneliness, how I longed for the enveloping warmness of your soft and pliable flesh! But I held myself firm to my purpose, for by then my plan was complete.

The next day I visited you at the man-compound. How proud and attractive you looked, how you stood out in beauty from the so poorly formed male specimens of Frth's impoverished race.

I brought to you that day the richest, most pungently flavored foods to be found in Frth. Day by day I tempted you to eat, adding pound after pound of handsomeness to your already perfect body. The Matriarch watched my every move jealously, but with a secret smile. For she planned to have you for herself. That, I and all my sisters understood.

And so I let her watch and smile, for she knew nothing of my plan. And I, alone, knew that she would be forced to accept one of the shabby, over-muscular Frthian males in your place. How I hated her.

For three long months I fed you. Then, one morning, the Matriarch stopped me as I came away from the man-compound.

"Why do you waste so much of your time and company on the foreign man-god?" she asked me tauntingly, a twisted grin on her face. "Do you not realize that in just two more nights the mating season will begin and the man-compound will be opened to all the eligible women in Frth?"

"I do this because I love him, Most Venerable One, and because I cannot do otherwise, no matter what the outcome."

"Ah, it is well. You are young and fleet of foot. Perhaps you will outdistance the others after all," she said.

But I knew it to be a lie. She would never have allowed you in the open competition. However, I did not care. For I alone knew that you would be mine long before then.

LATE that evening I slipped away from my dwelling and hid beside the man-compound where you were an unwilling prisoner. The guards were few, for all but one or two were resting well for the festivities that would begin the following night. All that night they would spend in sacred dancing and celebration, and with the first rays of the sun the next morning, the doors to the man-compound would he opened to them. This year's pitiful crop of just-maturing males would be up for competition, going to the fleetest of the eligible women.

I waited for hours, hesitantly, frightened, wondering if my plan would work.

And then, I felt creep over me the wonderful sensation of womanhood, and I knew I had won!

I had outguessed the Matriarch! She had forgotten that when a woman of our race first comes to maturity, the mating cycle is often out of harmony with the rest of our group. Usually it begins a full two days early! I was mature, ready for you a full two days before the Old One had thought I would be!

With all the stealth at my command I overcame the two of my sisters guarding the compound. I threw open the wooden gate and walked boldly into your pen.

You looked at me in surprise, but when you saw it was I, your look changed to *horror*. Oh, that I could make you understand how this thrilled and delighted me! I reached out to your mind, and sharing your thoughts, I understood and was happy.

For the males in the compound had told you something of the finale of our fertility rites! You had not comprehended all of what they had said, your mind was in confusion, but you had gathered enough to be terribly frightened.

"Josephine," you cried out, "you can't! Not me! You don't want me, Josephine, you—you—*cannibal!*"

I opened my arms to embrace you, but you ducked and squirmed away from me and fled screaming from the compound, the layers of fat bouncing as you waddled rapidly into the night.

THANKFUL beyond words I set out slowly to follow you. For this was as it had to be. Frthian males must always run from the females, or the mating cycle cannot come to fullness.

The secretions that my body carries are poisonous under normal circumstances. But, when administered to a male who is completely fatigued, to a male who has run for so many hours that he cannot move another step, the poisons do not kill. Instead, they create a suspended animation.

If you had not discovered just enough to flee when you saw me, you would have been dead by now. For I could not have long controlled my passions. Then I, too, would have died from the premature use of the poisons.

But it is hours now since you have fled from me through the blue darkness of the forests. How carefully, how devotedly I have followed you, pacing your every step, anticipating your every movement, listening to your fat screams with infinite delight.

Soon it will be time and I will catch up with you. The sheaths of my fangs will retract, and I will give to you the searing kiss of a fully matured woman. And slowly, softly, you will collapse in my arms.

Gently I will pick you up and carry you back to our dwelling. I will rest your body well on the bier of honor, making you as comfortable as possible.

And then, after the mating cycle is completed, we will wait.

As I go about my daily tasks, moving around your resting-place, my mind will be with yours constantly, sharing your every thought. For your mind will be unaffected by the paralysis of your body.

Linked together mentally we'll come to know the intimate secrets of the origin of new life. Thus united we will experience the glorious day when the eggs that I have laid break open and our children emerge to feed upon your rich flesh.

We will feel, as if we were one, our offspring as they burrow through your tissues, drawing sustenance from your ampleness.

How proud, how happy you will be to feel them growing larger, growing stronger, within you every day! And over the long, long months I will share with you these exquisite sensations.

Oh, you will father so many strong children!

NOW it is time. You are lying on the ground beside me, panting. I feel the great weariness of you. I see the great shiningness in your eyes—and I am ready.

Do not fight me—this part is so swift! Just one deep kiss, one gentle nip you will not even feel, a long caress of love…

Oh, my darling, I love you so!

THE END

SA'ANTHA

By E. Everett Evans

Suddenly he remembered the words of call that would bring the spirit of the woods to him again.

THE humming tires sang a new song as the big sedan was turned into the graveled side-road leading to the old homestead. They awakened old echoes in the benumbed, deadened mind of young Jon Maryth, and he roused a bit.

"Will this be the joyous homecoming, about which I've dreamed so many years?" his thoughts questioned. "Or is life over for me, with no hope of joy left?"

He knew a slight sense of guilt at coming back, seeking, so quickly after the untimely death of his parents in that terrible train wreck from which he had so providentially escaped. But his *need* was so great...his *beliefs* as strong as ever.

"But it cannot be," he thought almost savagely, "that Lachesis is such a cosmic jester, to spin so sorry a tapestry for me. Those tangled threads must have a meeting again!"

The xylophone-rattle of the car crossing the plank flooring of the well-remembered little covered wooden bridge again roused Jon from his memories, and he sat up quickly to peer through the car window.

And there—there in the swiftly nearing distance—was the great stand of timber—the Big Wood. There came a lightness, a sense of joy and complete happiness in his heart for a brief instant...then doubt forced it away.

Would She be there? It had been so long. But She *must* be! He knew it was a true memory, not a childish delusion as his parents insisted and, which, since he refused to admit their claims, had led them to move to the distant city so he could forget, as he grew older.

As though he ever would, or could, forget *Her!*

"It won't be long now, Honey," Mammy Martha's kindly old voice broke into his reflections, "but I still think it's wrong of you to come back here like this."

Jon Maryth grunted in annoyance even as Uncle Girard spoke sharply to his wife, beside him in the front seat. "You hush, now, Mammy. 'Member, we promised Mister Jon not to say anything 'gainst his wishing."

Sight of the big old New England farmhouse brought such rush of memories that Jon's frail body shook with emotion. For the moment he forgot even his purpose as pictures of the happy times with Dad and Mom here came welling into his mind, filling his eyes with tears. For he had loved them so much, and the ache of their passing was heavy on his heart. He knew, now, that they had acted in good faith and for what they thought his best interests in taking him away. Oh, if they could only have *believed!*

Much as he desired to go to Her at once, Maryth knew he was far too weak to make the attempt after this long automobile ride. He was thankful for Uncle Girard's strong arms that almost carried him up the broad, winding stairs to the well-remembered room, and helped him undress and get into the old four-poster bed.

While the two faithful old colored servitors scurried about unpacking and righting the long-unused house, Maryth lay quietly, his eyes seeking out the old curios and keepsakes in the room. A long hour dragged its slow seconds past him without his moving. He lapsed into that curious sort of trance that is neither waking nor sleeping, and memory dug back into his boyhood here on the farm.

One special day nudged itself into clearer picturization.

IT WAS one of those warm, lazy summer afternoons in the country when the whole world is taking a siesta. Only the little things, such as bees, ants, butterflies and small boys, were active.

Young Jon Maryth, in knickers and blouse, head bared to the tanning sun, idled through the clover field, on his way to the Big Wood, his favorite playing place. His bare feet *squilched* in the dust of the field. Occasionally he broke off a sprig of fragrant clover between his first and big toes, bringing it up to his nose to smell, while standing balanced acrobatically on one leg.

There was a cool mustiness to the Big Wood that he loved. The leafy canopy of boughs kept out the burning sun, the still, mossy paths between the trees were all roads leading to romantic places.

He stopped at the slippery elm tree to cut off a piece of the savory inner bark, which he chewed as he ambled along.

His mind drifted into the spinning of tales of high adventure in the Faroff Lands, as his feet slowly bore him towards the little, bubbling spring in a clearing he knew, near the center of the Wood. The water there, always cool and sweet, would taste so good on this hot summer day.

He was almost upon the spring when he saw *Her* sitting a little way from it, dabbling her naked feet in the little rivulet that carried the overflow away from the spring pool.

Jon stopped short, then jumped behind a great spruce, his head cocked so he could peer out from behind his hiding place, to see without being seen. At first he could see only that it was a woman, dressed in some sort of a leaf-green robe, of some filmy material he did not know.

She did not seem aware of him, was relaxed and carefree. There was a peculiar sound in the air, which the boy soon identified as a trilling hum that he knew she was making. A lilting little song of pure joy, without words nor need of them. It made a happy little thrill run all through him.

Carefully he crept nearer, edging his way from tree-bole to stump to bush. Finally he was not more than a dozen feet away. Ordinarily shy in front of strangers, he wanted desperately to see her face. He could not have told why. Women, as such, did not interest him, except his beautiful mother, and genial old Martha, his colored Mammy.

But he felt a strange, urgent desire to see this woman's face. He wished she would turn, yet was afraid that if she did she would see him and make him go away. He didn't know who she was or could be. He had never seen anyone here before, certainly not anyone dressed like that.

Why'd she wear such funny clothes, he wondered? But they were kinda pretty, he decided.

THEN, suddenly she did turn her head, and he caught almost a full view of her. A gasp of surprise escaped him at the piquant beauty of that heart-shaped face with its little pointed chin, so different from any other he had ever seen.

At that gasp, slight though it was, she leaped to her feet in one graceful motion, stood poised as though ready for instant flight, glancing quickly all about. Almost at once she spotted him, stood looking at him, at first half-afraid, then puzzled, then with a friendly smile as she saw but a small, barelegged, tousled-haired, astonished boy.

"Hello, Human," she said, and he wondered briefly at the wording.

"'Lo," he replied, sidling nearer. Then, after a long pause, he blurted, "you're pretty."

She smiled at the compliment, turned and sat down again with the most graceful ease he had ever seen. She beckoned. "Come, sit before me. The water is cool on one's feet."

When, as dusk was descending, he heard the distant clangor of the supper bell, he reluctantly rose. "I have to go now, Lady. Can I come and see you again and you can tell me more stories about those Old Ones?"

"Of course, Boy, I want you to come and see me often." Her hand caressed him with a curiously sensitive touch, from which he broke away to race back across the fields, bursting with his tremendous news.

At the table he spilled it out in a spate of words that came so swiftly his parents could not at first even understand, and forced him to calm down a bit and talk slower.

Again he told about the wonderful Beautiful Lady he had met in the Big Wood, how kind She was, how thrilling the tales She told him.

He only half-noticed the puzzled glances Dad and Mom exchanged as he talked, but gradually their faces lightened. When he finished Dad threw back his head and laughed uproariously...and Jon knew a sudden sinking sensation. Why, Dad had *never* laughed at him before. He sank deep into his chair, the hand holding his fork hesitated, then laid it down again, the piece of roast untouched.

"You fell asleep by the spring, and dreamed it all, Son," Dad said, and Mom added, "It's from some old story you've read."

"But I wasn't asleep and I didn't dream it," he insisted. "I wasn't even up to the spring when I first saw Her, and She was too real and we did talk all afternoon," and again that hurt feeling when he saw they did not believe him.

Rather, they talked earnestly about the impossibility of such a happening, and after awhile, so plausible were their words, and so much did he trust them, there came the first tinges of doubt and he went to bed wondering if it might not, after all, have been a dream.

To the young man now remembering, there seemed to be something he could not quite recall. It seemed to have to do with words, with important words he had forgotten. Nor could he wring further remembrance from his ill mind...

But the next day, unwilling to disbelieve what he was so sure was truth, he hesitantly ventured back to the Big Wood again, and there at the spring he found Her once more, waiting for him to come, trembling with anxiety lest he fail Her.

Sitting by Her side beneath the great oak, he told Her of his parents' disbelief, of their mocking laughter.

"It is always the way, Boy," she said sadly but tenderly. "Only those with the Spirit of Youth within can one ever see or know us." And when he did not understand, She turned the matter aside by beginning another tale of the Long Ago.

That night he again tried to persuade his parents about the realness of his Beautiful Lady, but they still would not believe, and at last Dad became angry with him for the first time he could remember, and sternly forbade him talking about it ever again.

But it is not in boy nature to keep silent, and he talked, over and over, and more and more he met with antagonism, harsh words and even whippings.

Still Jon managed to see Her almost daily, and had it not been for Her comforting love and sweetness, the boy felt he would die...or run away.

The coming of Winter and the deep snows made it impossible for him to go to the Big Wood to meet Her, and as the weeks sped by he ceased talking about Her, much to his parents' relief.

But never, for even an hour, did he forget.

Anxiously he waited for the snows to melt, and the first warm Saturday morning of Spring he ran at top speed back to the spring in the Big Wood, and there he found Her again, and their happy hours together resumed...while the hours at home grew more troubled.

ONE day there had been a stranger at the house, who had talked with Jon for hours, asking all sorts of silly questions.

Then, a week later, Jon Maryth was ordered into the car with his parents, and soon found himself on a train, and at last in the new home in the distant city where he was to live until this recent, sudden death of his parents released him to return to the beloved farm home.

But that distance had not made him forget, as his parents had hoped. The crushing blow of his forcible separation from his beloved Beautiful Lady—without even a chance to say goodbye or tell Her he was being taken away—made him sullen, brooding, his health undermined by the weakness and despair of his spirit. Now he was invalid, although he could get around to some extent if he did not exert himself too much.

Yes, Jon Maryth remembered that first meeting so well. Remembered, too, the countless others…and all they had meant to him. How She had…

UNCLE GIRARD interrupted his daydreaming just then, coming with a tray heaped with tempting viands Mammy Martha had prepared to tempt his never-too-good appetite.

As he picked at his food, the noise of the countryside symphony tuning up for its evening concert was borne through the open window on the gentle evening breeze. He heard once more with delight the violin-pizzicati of the crickets and cicadas, the strident oboe-tones of the tree-toads, the booming bassoon-notes of the bullfrogs in the little pond behind the big barn, the drumming rumble of ruffed grouse from the distant Wood.

Immediately after breakfast, in spite of protests from the loving two who did not think he was strong enough either for the long walk or the emotional excitement, he started out. Past the back of the house he went, past the creamery and the big barn, walking slowly but purposefully down the cow-lane towards the fields.

As he ambled through the sweet alfalfa, reveling in the sights and smells that brought boyhood closer every second, Jon Maryth considered that perhaps it was good to be alive after all; that perhaps there still was something to live for.

Especially since he would see Her in a few minutes.

At last he reached the edge of the Big Wood. How familiar it was. Ah, there was the path. Well, hiya, old Shagbark Hickory! Long time no see…hello, Walnut, have to come get some of your nuts this Fall…and my pretty twins, the Silver Poplars. Beautiful as ever, aren't you—and as proud of your beauty…good old Mister Slip'ry Elm; got to have a piece of your tasty bark.

Deeper, deeper into the cool loveliness of the well-remembered place, past all his old familiar tree friends, Jon Maryth went with quickening pace, an inner excitement seeming to bring back his youthful strength. And there, just ahead, he spied the little spring.

"Lady! *Lady!*" he shouted then, "It's Jon, come to see you again! Where are you, Lady! Are you glad to see your little Jon again?"

He was at the spring now, still calling, looking eagerly all about, expecting every moment to see her come running down an aisle between the great trees. In his mind's eye he could see her again so plainly, each line of her slim, willowy figure...the long, flowing hair the color of young brown bark...the pansy-violet eyes with their lights of laughter and love of life and wisdom. It was so he had first seen Her, clad in flowing, leaf-green robes; it was so he had seen her almost daily for a year and a half, except during that winter.

"Lady! Beautiful Lady! Hurry! It's Jon!" In his excitement he peered about, running now this way, now that, seeking her.

But she did not appear, nowhere could he see her.

Alarmed and worried now, he rushed through the Big Wood, calling aloud anxiously seeking her in its remotest depths, yet every few moments running back into the clearing by the spring, to see if she had appeared there.

His legs failed him at last. He sank, panting, onto the mossy bank beneath the big oak by the spring. It couldn't be that she had moved away.

She *belonged* there, he knew. For he knew now what she was, why she fitted so naturally into this woodland scene.

His face blanched and his breath stopped at a horrid thought. Dead? Oh, *no!* It simply was not possible. Not his Beautiful Lady, so much alive that she seemed life itself! No. He must not—*he would not*—believe she, too, had thus been torn from him. And yet, when he examined it, he could see that the great oak was past its prime, that in many places it was rotted and with many dying branches.

Stupored, he turned and threw himself at full length, face down on the soft, sweet moss, crying his despair, his disappointment, his need of her.

Try to forget, the wind whispered in his ears and in his mind. But he could never forget the vastness of his loss. Not remember Mom's sweetness, her loving tenderness and her care; not remember Dad's flashing, scintillant mind, his usual good-humored steadiness; not remember his Beautiful Lady's entrancing face and vibrant form, the wonderful tales she had told him of people and events when the world was young; the many things about Nature she had taught him with a clearness he had never been able to comprehend about the things he had merely studied in school?

Foolish wind to counsel him thus.

A swift encroaching fog of blackness enveloped and blotted out his every sense.

JON MARYTH came back to full consciousness to discover himself lying in his own bed, with the late afternoon light showing through his window. "What th'?" he muttered, and tried to raise up but found himself unable to do so. He wondered how long he had been sick this time, to get that weak.

He turned his head on the pillow, saw several half-emptied bottles of medicine on the little table nearby, that told their own story.

"Mammy!" he yelled, and was surprised how weak and small his voice was. But she must have been near and heard him even so, for in a moment she came bustling in, beaming.

"Oh, Mister Jon, it's so good to see you awake again and looking like you knew what was going on," she cried as she came to his side and stooped down to kiss him.

"How long have I been sick, Mammy?"

"'Bout eight days, Honey. Uncle Girard and the farm man found you out there in the woods, burning up with fever, late that night when you didn't come home. We was mighty scared for three, four days, but ol' Doc Fergerson he said he'd pull you through all right, and praise th' Lord, he shore did."

"Well, I'm still awfully weak, and mighty hungry. Could I have some broth...or something?"

She laughed happy assent, as she went to the door and hollered to Uncle Girard to "bring Mister Jon some of that soup!"

While he was sipping it, the two old servants watching him in fond joy, told him something of his illness, and that for a couple of days he was really out of his head.

"Can you remember what it was you wanted, Honey?" Mammy asked anxiously. "You seemed so almighty worried about something, or wanting somebody. You kept calling out 'Hello, Sanna,' or something like that, as though you…"

Jon had been digesting that, now its true import struck him all at once. His excitement raised both his body and his voice.

"Say that again, Mammy!" he shouted, eyes agleam with the beginning of understanding and remembrance. "Say what you just now said I said!"

"Why, Honey, I just said you kept calling for somebody by the name of Sanna; you kept yelling 'Hello, Sanna,' like you wanted 'em to come and help you."

"Of course," he said, mostly to himself, striking his forehead with the heel of his hand. "How stupid of me to forget. No wonder She didn't come when I called." He turned to them. "It wasn't 'Hello, Sanna' I was saying, Mammy. It was *"Aillau, Sa'antha,'* and that's what I was trying so hard to remember. Those are the words my Beautiful Lady taught me, by which to call her."

Ignoring their questions about this, he slowly raised himself to a full sitting position, then slid his feet out from under the covers and into his slippers, lying on the floor beside his bed. Slowly he rose and stood holding the bedpost for a moment while his head cleared. Then he reached for his robe.

"What you think you're doing, Honey?" Mammy asked, and Uncle Girard came forward as though to stop him.

He ignored them, however. When they would have restrained him, he first motioned them away, and then pushed angrily against them with unexpected strength. And was gone from the room.

Down the broad stairs he went, his purpose seeming to give him new vigor with each foot of progress made. Through the door and into the yard, shivering a bit, noting the sky was thickly overcast now, that there was the feel of rain in the air. He headed for the shed-garage, got into his car, backed it out, and headed it down the lane. He heard Uncle Girard call, saw him running forward, but neither answered nor waited.

TOO impatient to spend the time and energy opening it, he crashed through the gate leading into the alfalfa field, leaving splintered wreckage behind him. Out across the rough, uneven field he thundered, bumping and rocking so he could hardly control the weaving of the big car. At the edge of the Big Wood he climbed out of the car without waiting to turn off the ignition.

The rain was coming down hard now, and thunder and lightning were adding to the din. But Maryth did not heed them. He trotted as fast as his trembling legs would bear him, towards the little clearing and the spring, calling out constantly as he ran, *"Aillau! Aillau, Sa'antha!* It is young Jon coming back to you! *Aillau Sa'antha!"*

He was nearly at the spring now, stumbling in his weakness, yet his anxiety and purpose compelling him on. His eyes searched eagerly ahead in every direction, though his voice seemed hardly audible above the fury of the storm.

He fell face downward on the path, and when his tired and worn muscles proved unequal to the task of raising his body upright once more, crawled forward, painfully, on hands and knees, still calling into the night and storm, *"Aillau! Aillau, Sa'antha!"*

Suddenly he saw Her, saw his Sa'antha step out of—not from behind, but actually *out of*—the big oak under which they had sat so often.

He called again, and She came close to him, looking down. She gazed puzzledly a moment, then an awareness grew that this strange young man was in reality the same human boy she had known and loved years ago...for whom she still grieved. Sa'antha uttered a cry of joy, then had her arms about him, lifting him, supporting him, leading him under the shelter of the great oak where, miraculously it seemed to him, no rain was falling now. Gently she eased his tired, aching body onto the soft mossy bank, his head softly cradled against her.

"Sa'antha, my lovely, Beautiful Lady. It's been so long...and I've been so lonely."

She murmured soft words, alien words, but comforting to his heart, and bringing peace and contentment once more. More quietly, then, he told her how he had been taken by his parents to live in that distant city, without even the chance of coming to bid Her farewell and explain.

"I cried, too, when you suddenly stopped coming," Sa'antha said gently. "My poor old oak has nearly died, I've neglected it so, grieving for you.

He told her of his illness, his continual grieving for her. Brokenly he related the death of his parents, and of his resolve immediately afterwards to come seeking her. Of his daydreams of remembrance of her, of his search, and how he had forgotten *the words of call,* of his illness when he could not find her and how his subconscious had remembered during his delirium.

"Can we not always be together now?" he begged. "It is only with you that I'll ever know true happiness and life. We can be, can't we?"

"I'd like that as much as you," she responded, and was silent, thoughtful for a long moment, while the storm raged about them. Then she nodded as though in decision and, rising to her feet, moved out into the storm-swept clearing.

Jon could hear her praying to the wind and the rain and the earth and the sky, asking that they two might be always together, that they need never part.

The young man staggered to his feet and moved out beside her. He joined his prayers to hers, with all his faith, with all his desire and need.

And then it happened. His sight gradually blurred, he could no longer see distinctly. There was a curious stiffening feeling in his body. He glanced down and saw a tender sprig of green bud starting from one of his fingers, then another and another. The bud swelled and burst, showing fine, young leaves of green.

The rain was falling harder now, and as it fell he could feel it washing away his clothing, washing away his mortality.

Dimly, he heard a shout from the distance, and he raised his fast-dimming eyes to see a figure he guessed must be Uncle Girard, running toward the spring. The old man had followed in spite of the storm. Jon felt a moment of sorrowful compunction for the grief his passing would bring, but knew that this was best.

Sa'antha was still praying, her voice no longer audible in his ears…yet he heard it still inside his mind, with his rapidly changing senses—heard and now understood her words. Maryth could perceive that the earth, the rain, the wind and the sky were listening, were sympathetic, were assisting.

The earth piled about his feet, and he could feel rootlets groping from his trembling flesh into the cool sweetness of the friendly soil.

His arms were now upraised, bark-covered, budding branches, his height increasing rapidly, his human senses subtly dissolving into newer, more ethereal forms.

The wind blew about them. The two oaks touched in the raining wind. The last vestige of Jon Maryth's mortality dissolved and rained in droplets to the warm earth, even as Uncle Girard, running still, slipped and started to fall, but caught himself against the new young tree.

The oak seemed to writhe. Girard stared at him, at the tree, then looked away, crying to the raining wilderness, "Mister Jon!"

Running again, he vanished away, while the rain fell steadily upon the trees and their leaves rustled quietly, one against the other, as Sa'antha entered her new home.

THE END

TWICE TO DIE

By Rog Phillips

For some, it is said, there can be solace in death... But what of those who once dead, find that they must die again?

I HAD some trouble getting my wallet back in my hip pocket. The zipper handle on it stuck to the corner of the lining, leaving the wallet dangling, half in half out. By the time I had untangled it and rose from the table the rest of the fellows were out of sight.

It was in the Old Heidelberg, the most exclusive restaurant in the block, which is about all I would say for exclusiveness in Chicago where *every* hash house aims, but just misses, exclusiveness. The Old Heidelberg's bid for fame was its rule that every customer must wear a coat.

I had just moved to Chicago from the west coast. I'm a writer, and I wanted to be nearer the markets for my stories. So far, I had only found a place where I could stay for four weeks while a guy who couldn't afford to take a vacation and pay rent at the same time had sublet his apartment to me while he was gone.

Ye editor, two fellow craftsmen, and I had lunched at the Old Heidelberg. I hurried as quickly as good taste would permit to catch up with them before they got too far. I wasn't quite sure which way the office was from any place three blocks from it.

Then it happened. The entrance to the dining room is always crowded at lunch time with people who had not reserved a table in advance. They stand there and look at the empty tables with white and black reserved signs on them, growing more and more hungry, while the foresighted few straggle in and brush past them.

Hurrying, I started through the crowd at the door. Suddenly a vision of feminine clothing, hat, and motion appeared in front of me. Too late I put on the brakes.

As her body collided with mine, and a tide of subtly pleasant perfume brushed into my nostrils, I felt a tingling shock. Instinctively I put my hands on her shoulders to steady her. The flood of words that rushed to my lips, the apology I had intended to make for my clumsiness, stopped in my throat as her head raised and her eyes met mine.

I don't know how long I stood there, oblivious of the people that crowded against me on all sides, my hands resting on her shoulders, my eyes looking into those pools of enchanting magic half hidden by an ethereal veil of golden lashes, breathing the faint aura of a perfume that I was sure no store had ever sold over the counter, my brain paralyzed and my body tingling in every cell. Time stood still.

But when my senses did return with a rush and I took my hands away with a muttered apology and stepped aside to allow her to pass, I was vaguely aware that no one around us had noticed anything out of the ordinary.

Stepping out onto the sidewalk I hurried past the strolling crowds, catching up with my luncheon companions. The vision of that haunting smile, the magic of those clear, blue-green eyes, the intoxication of that faint perfume, sank themselves into my soul, to fill it with the memory of an experience like none other I had ever known, and to create an emptiness like none I had ever known. An emptiness that could only be filled in one way.

I half turned, debating whether I should go back and seize the opportunity while it was yet there. But I didn't. I went to the office and spent the afternoon kicking myself for not having done so.

To cover my state of mind I buried my face in a magazine, letting my eyes rest on the pages and my mind wander in speculation, again living the intoxicating experience and thrilling to the vibrant touch of those shoulders, the hypnotic ecstasy of those eyes.

"Hey, Jack," my reverie was shattered by the voice of Bill Fleming. "Here's a chance for you to get a place to stay. Some rich guy wants a gatekeeper."

"Let's see it," I growled, taking the paper from him and reading where he pointed.

The ad read, "Wanted, Gate keeper. Cottage furnished. Prefer elderly man on pension." The address was just off of North Shore Drive, in the section where every other house was over a century old, surrounded by a high stone fence, entrance to the grounds being made through ornamental iron gates set in the walls.

I had been out that way before and remembered some of them. I had even remarked about the gatekeeper's cottages being much nicer looking than some of the more modern homes in the newer sections.

THE possibilities struck me at once. A place to stay, in surroundings that would surely bring to mind numberless ideas for stories. The added advantage of no rent to pay. An occasional bell to answer would be the only drawback. Ha! I would work for nothing to get the job.

"Do you think I should go over to the costumers and get a white wig and beard, and maybe a cane, to apply for the job?" I asked Bill.

"I don't know," he answered. "Why don't you try it on the level. If that fails, *then* get the wig and cane."

"O.K.," I answered with a broad grin. "See you later."

The place was just as I had pictured it would be. In fact, I had a vague remembrance of having seen it before; perhaps a picture somewhere. I pulled my Buick to the curb near the driveway that led through the black iron lattice work of the gates and curved through the trees to the side of the huge, stone mansion, about fifty yards back from the street.

A stone archway separated the gate of the footpath from the driveway gates. Set in the iron frame was a small push-button. I pressed it and whistled a tune while waiting for a response.

Five minutes later no one had showed up, so I tried the gate. It swung open at my touch.

The path swung away from the driveway and wound around a large flowerbed, branching when it reached the house. I took the branch that led to the rear. Through the windows as I passed them the house seemed deserted. High-ceilinged rooms, nicely furnished in old stuff that was in keeping with the exterior. Paintings on the walls. But not a soul in any of them.

I don't know why, but I had expected a cluttered backyard and a large back porch with a roof over it. Instead, the back of the house looked no different than the sides. The driveway on the other end of the back wall spread out to cover the entire front of a four-car garage generously, a narrow path leading from it in a straight line to join the one I stood on at the back door. And the door itself was an ordinary, weathered green, windowless one set into the stone wall of the house at almost ground level, a single concrete step setting it away from the sidewalk.

The large garage, set diagonally about thirty feet from the far corner of the house, only accentuated the bareness and monotony of the back lawn, which stretched with perfect flatness to the rear wall of the grounds, a half dozen large, unkempt trees rooted haphazardly in a half dead, closely cropped lawn.

Once more I pressed a button, this time recessed in the wooden frame of the doorway. Inside I heard a single, melodious bong from a muted chime.

"The chime, at least, is twentieth century stuff," I thought. By now I felt too subdued by the immensity and atmosphere of lifelessness of the three-storied, mansford-roofed, stone building to whistle. And almost at once I heard movement inside. The sound of leather heels against wooden floor came nearer. It stopped for so long before the door swung open that I looked curiously about, expecting to see some sort of a peep hole through which a visitor could be spied upon unobserved from inside.

Then the door opened. A woman in her forties, dressed in a black uniform dress, a small square of white apron tied around her waist, looked up at me questioningly.

I pointed to the newspaper I held in my hand and said, "I've come about the ad for a gatekeeper. Is the position still open?"

"Just a minute, sir," the woman said. She started to close the door, then hesitated and said, "Won't you come inside, please?"

WITH a muttered "Thank you" I took off my hat and stepped through the doorway. It was a short, service hallway. I stood there uncomfortably while the maid went through the door at the end of the hall, closing it softly behind her, with the funereal quiet of an undertaker.

Almost immediately she returned, holding the door open and saying, "Won't you step this way, please?"

Her smile—in fact her whole face and figure could only be described by one word, Expressionless.

I stepped past her onto a thick carpeted floor. The room was large, and across the room, seated in a high-backed upholstered chair from some forgotten era, was a small, fragile looking, white haired lady. Her modern dress, whose replica I had seen in many store windows, seemed almost out of place.

She remained seated, a polite smile on her wrinkled face. I noted absently that she did have her powder on smooth.

I inclined my head in a gesture of respect for the years of the lady and her house.

"You are calling about the position for someone else?" she asked curiously.

"No. For myself," I replied. "You see, there is such a housing shortage, and I am a writer. I could both fulfill the duties of gatekeeper and write my stories."

She frowned over this. I tried to look past her eyes and sense what she was thinking. There seemed almost an emptiness, as if the shell of the woman only was there and the spirit had departed some time years ago, unnoticed.

"Would you like to leave your address?" she asked suddenly. "If we decide to accept you we can get in touch with you."

With a feeling of relief I hastily wrote my phone number and address on a sheet out of my pocket note pad. I felt, or rather hoped, that this stall meant I wouldn't be hired.

The place seemed all right, but there was—well, something I could only sense vaguely, that didn't seem right. She accepted the proffered sheet of notepaper with an air of dismissal. I didn't need any more of a hint. Repeating my polite nod and accompanying it with a smile, I turned and left the way I had come. The maid was nowhere in sight as I walked down the back hall and stepped out onto the sidewalk once more. I retraced my steps to the front gate, glancing curiously at the gatekeeper's cottage on my way back to the car.

The cottage was nice appearing. A single story high roof and walls seeming too massive for such a small building, but in keeping with the big house. I started over to look through a window, then shrugged my shoulders and went through the gate. I wasn't going to get the job, so why bother?

It was too late to go back to the office, so I went to the apartment and spent the evening pounding out a few more pages of my latest yarn. Before I went to bed I had forgotten the whole thing, storing it in some mental corner where I could drag it out and set it into a story sometime.

A week passed. During that week I ate lunch regularly at the Old Heidelberg, hoping I would run into my dream again, with no success. I even had dinner there. But no soap. She didn't show up.

Also I pounded out a couple of thousand words a day, bowled a couple of evenings, and spent more and more time looking for a permanent place to stay. No luck there either. I could have found half a dozen sleeping rooms. But to take one would have been very expensive to a writer who needs a pleasant place to work and a reasonable amount of quiet during the day.

I HAD just about given up hope, and was thinking ruefully of the long trip back to the coast. Just about, but not quite. I would rent a sleeping room and look in other cities near Chicago before doing that.

Then the phone rang. Bill Flemming had called me up an hour previously. I hadn't had any "feelings" about that. There was no tangible reason why I should hesitate this time. The ring was no different. But I hesitated, a feeling of something causing me to hesitate. A feeling something like a hunch.

The voice on the other end of the phone was that of the old lady who had taken my number. I heard her ask for me, replied that I was Jack Marley, and heard her say that she had decided to accept my application.

Then I was caught up in a maze of details in which I didn't have time to do much thinking. I snapped out of it finally, relaxed in a somewhat moth-eaten armchair, firmly ensconced in the gatekeeper's cottage, before a cheery fire I had built in the huge stone fireplace to clear out the dampness.

Even yet I can't remember all the details of moving. One minute I was hesitating about answering the phone. The next, with only a vague sense of passage of time and hurry of events, I was looking into the flames of the fire and trying to convince myself that I was not dreaming.

I hadn't seen the old lady. The maid had met me and given me the key to the cottage. I had been told I could park my car in the garage in the stall at the extreme right, and from then on I had been completely ignored.

The parting shot of the maid had been, "Breakfast for the servants is promptly at seven."

"Servant!" I had muttered to myself. "I'll bet I make more money than the Mawster." The memory of a cold-hearted Chicago, which had locked its doors on everyone not already "in" forced me to be a good boy, and I merely smiled, trying to show a nonexistent gratitude.

It was after dark when I finally brought the last load of papers, typewriters, books, and manuscript copies and stuffed them away in closets so that I could unpack them later at my leisure. I had eaten my dinner on the way out with the last load, so after parking the car in its stall and glancing curiously around the garage, I had built the fire and relaxed.

The sky had been threatening all day. The radio had predicted a storm during the night. While I sat before the fireplace getting more and more drowsy the windows occasionally lit up with the light of heat lightning. But when I finally stood up and crossed the room to the bedroom door, there still had been not a single drop of rain.

I DON'T know when I woke up. The thunder, which awakened me, was still crashing in the sky. It seemed directly overhead and very close, and during the moments when the prolonged blast of sound was momentarily stilled I could hear the downpour of rain as it beat against the roof and the ground outside.

I lay there and tossed about, unable to go back to sleep. Finally I arose and lit a cigarette. The French window I had opened for ventilation had blown shut, so I crossed the room to open it.

I pushed it open and leaned out, looking for some sign of a hook to keep it open. Lightning flashed across the sky through the trees, and the grounds were lit up so that every detail stood out, in sharp clarity.

The rain was coming down in large drops that bounced as they hit the ground. The large house, its windows dark and mysterious, stood like a huge, immovable, timeless monument, squatting above the casket of some Titan who had lived in ages gone by.

But my eyes were arrested by something more. Standing in the rain, her arms upraised as if in supplication, was a girl. Her face was raised into the rain. She stood in profile, her long, sheer white dress molding her figure in revealing detail, the wind whipping it out into waving streamers behind.

The vision beat into my brain with sharp vividness, and then was gone as the sky ceased its unloosing of titanic electric force and became dark.

I couldn't think. My eyes bored through the night, trying by sheer force of will to pierce the rain-drenched darkness. And the shock, the terrible shock of seeing the girl in the rain, drenched undoubtedly to the skin, in attire which no one in their right mind would wear *if they were awake*, was a minor thing compared to the realization that it was the girl I had met in the Old Heidelberg!

Suddenly I turned and stumbled through the darkness of the room toward the door. My frantic haste made me clumsy and I cursed silently as I stumbled against a chair. There was no time to remember where the light switches were.

I burst into the living room. The still burning fire on the hearth sent feeble, but adequate rays of light through the room.

In bare feet, clad only in broadcloth pajamas, I flung open the door and dashed into the rain, running down the path in the general direction of the girl. Lightning cascaded across the sky constantly, revealing the girl to still be there, her figure as revealed by the flashes, appearing like an image in the old flicker movies. And overhead the thunder beat a mad, unworldy rhythm of sound. It dominated the pounding of my heart, the harsh panting of my breath, and the beat of my feet against the rain-drenched path.

As I neared her she seemed to sense my presence, half-turning toward me, a pale smile on her lips. I put my arm around her slim waist and picked her up. Her arms went around my shoulders and her eyes sought mine as the thunder and the lightning beat a deafening, blinding crescendo.

My lips met hers crushingly, and my soul tottered on the brink of the Abyss, flayed by the pounding of the storm, shaken by the ecstasy of that kiss, drunk with a madness of emotion so strong, so overpowering and intense that the very pain of it was ecstatic, overpowering pleasure.

Then sanity returned. My lips broke away from hers. The intermittent light showed the whiteness of her slim, lovely form was bluish from exposure. I felt her trembling.

I turned and stumbled back toward the cottage. In the darkness her lips again sought mine, feverishly. I was lost in indescribable madness, my mind whirling feverishly in the passion of her lips, my feet moving unsteadily forward.

With no warning blackness enveloped me.

MY EYES opened slowly. I was in the living room of the cottage. The fire in the fireplace was burning brightly and standing before it, his back turned to me, was a man. His dark suit coat fitted tightly over the heavily muscled shoulders. The light grey, pin-stripe trousers hung gracefully from slim hips, their unspoiled creases dropping to the tops of brown shoes.

The closely cropped black head hinted at a high forehead, and the small ears hugged the side of the head closely.

My eyes darted around the room. No one else was there. I glanced down. I was in the chair I had occupied earlier in the evening. Under my bathrobe was a fresh pair of broadcloth pajamas. My skin felt warm and dry. And on my feet were my blue leather bedroom slippers.

There was a dull throbbing at the back of my head. I reached up with my hand and explored carefully. My hair was dry, but mussed, with the soft, clean feel to it that hair has after being washed and dried. In back was a very tender spot, slightly swollen.

I fished a cigarette out of the pack in my bathrobe pocket and a book of matches. The scratching of the match, or perhaps the light it made, caused the man to turn around. My hand shook violently as I tried to light the cigarette. It went out.

"Here, let me light it for you," the man said, coming forward, a look of concern on his face. He took the match folder from my unresisting fingers and bent over, and as I sucked deeply on the cigarette I noticed that his fingers were perfectly steady.

His clear brown eyes were calm. A shade of concern and pity blended into the habitual intellectual mold of his face. His forehead was high, his nose thin and finely formed. His chin just missed being square. There was power and breeding in his features, a self-assurance that is seldom found in any but foreigners.

The cut of his coat and the way he bore himself hinted at central Europe more than Chicago. And there had been just a shade of an accent in his rich baritone voice when he had spoken.

Suddenly the memory of the girl came back. It swept over me in a rushing tide, and the cigarette which I had been holding in my hand seared into the flesh as the emotion accompanying the return of memory constricted my fingers involuntarily.

An exclamation of pain escaped from my lips and I rubbed the hot coals from my palm onto my bathrobe, swearing fervently under my breath. But the pain cleared my brain of its cobwebs.

"Who *are* you?" I asked, half angrily.

"My name is Doctor Henry Blech," he said, pronouncing the ch with the prolonged German soft k sound. "I'll tell you a little about me if you care to listen."

"O.K.," I snapped. I pulled out another cigarette and this time I lit it successfully.

"I am a psychiatrist," Dr. Blech began. "Years ago I practiced in Vienna. I gained somewhat of a reputation." He shrugged his shoulders disparagingly. "The reputation spread to America. Perhaps some book I wrote had a little to do with that. I don't know.

"At any rate, in nineteen thirty-five I received an invitation to come to the United States in a consultive capacity on a certain case. A fellow practitioner of mine here in Chicago had something he considered unique in the history of psychiatry. He sent me the case history. I found that if his notes were accurate it was indeed something unique. So I dropped my practice temporarily and came.

"That was eleven years ago, and I am still here as you can see." He pulled out a slim cigarette case and lit a long, unusually slim cigarette.

WHILE he was doing that I was remembering that girl. I had been dimly conscious, even in my madness, that something was wrong. What was it? The expression on her face? Her being in the storm in such flimsy costume? The way her lips sought mine, and me a stranger who had suddenly loomed up in the night? All these things definitely pointed to insanity.

And yet, her eyes as I had looked in them that afternoon in the Old Heidelberg, had been sane. Completely sane and normal, in spite of the electrifying effect they had had on me.

And there was an underlying difference in the effect she had had on me then, and the effect she had had on me as she lay limp and unresisting in my arms, the storm beating against us. The storm that still raged outside.

I had sensed it subconsciously, but had been so overcome with madness and the single desire to get her in out of the storm and get help for her that I had not stopped to analyze those feelings then.

Now I was doing so. And suddenly the logical solution flashed into my mind.

"They are twins!" I exclaimed in triumph.

"Yes," and a look of startled surprise appeared on Dr. Blech's face. "But how did you know? You have more knowledge of the case than your—er, experience of an hour ago?"

Briefly I told him of meeting the girl at the Old Heidelberg. I explained my surprise at seeing what I thought to be the same girl as I looked at the raging storm from my bedroom window, and how I had gone to her rescue, dimly sensing she was not right, and losing myself in madness as she rested in my arms, her face so near.

"I didn't know then that it wasn't the same girl, but her twin," I concluded.

Dr. Blech had listened, a thoughtful, attentive expression on his face. After I ceased talking he seemed to be studying what I had said. Finally he spoke.

"You love this girl you met in the restaurant?" he asked.

"Yes!" I said defiantly. "Oh, I know it sounds screwy, to meet a girl only once, and then for only an instant. And to be so certain you are in love with her. But I'm certain. And I'm equally certain that she had the same feeling."

"Then let me tell you this," the doctor said. His whole demeanor had changed. His sensitive nostrils were flaring and his dark eyes held a fire of smoldering anger. "They are twins, *but they have only one body.*"

The shock of his words paralyzed me. I watched dumbly as he turned his broad back to me, trying visibly to control his emotions. Finally he turned again.

"I'll tell you the whole story," he resumed in a quieter voice. "You met Mrs. Andrews? Of course you did. She is the old lady whom you saw when you applied for the position of gatekeeper. She is the mother of the twins.

"She was fifty-three when they were born. That is unusual enough in itself. But to have twins at that age is even more rare. They were both girls, but one of them had died when in the partially completed stage of development that is arrived at when the embryo is about seven months old.

"The two embryos had developed so closely intertwined that in the month they had lain together while one of them was dead, the substance of the dead one had been partially absorbed into the living, and partly into the body of the mother herself.

"IT WILL remain a medical mystery how the living child survived in the presence of the toxic products of decay of the dead for so long. The mother herself was so far gone that for a long time the doctors in attendance had little hope of saving her life.

"But the child seemed healthy and normal, and even to have an unusual vitality and alertness. Or so the charts in the files of the attending physician lead us to believe.

"Nothing abnormal about the child was noticed for many years. When abnormality *did* develop, the parents and the nurse, whom you have also met, I believe, recalled that the girl had always, even as a baby, had 'spells' when she was utterly different.

"There seemed to be two distinct personalities developing in the child. At first both were entirely normal. That is assumed because the real trouble did not begin until the child had almost reached womanhood. And by then both personalities were developed and completely distinct.

"But then a struggle began. I believe that as the realization dawned upon each that love, marriage, and childbearing were just around the corner, so to speak, each determined to have the body to herself exclusively.

"Up until that period in life, each had been mainly concerned with intellectual pursuits, and each had tolerated the presence of the other because there was no real disadvantage to either in their sharing in the occupation of their physical body.

"As is always the case in any struggle, one of the two personalities or spirits was stronger than the other. I believe she was stronger because *she realized it was not rightfully her body*. In short, she was the soul of the dead twin, and had gone into the body of her living sister as they lay together in the womb of their mother."

The doctor paused in his story, tossing the stub of his cigarette into the fireplace with a vicious flick of his fingers he continued.

"Gradually the rightful owner of the body weakened, her reason slowly slipped away, she began to break under the constant attacks of her sister. Her periods of dominance became shorter and shorter.

"The parents could not understand what was going on, of course. When their daughter began to have fits of weeping and abnormalcy they consulted the leading psychiatrist in Chicago. He studied the case for several months, even having the girl in his sanitarium for a few months under close observation.

"Finally he pieced together the bits of the puzzle. He realized it was beyond his ability to effect a cure. He advised the parents to secure the services of the most outstanding psychiatrist in the world, warning them that even then, in his opinion, there was little hope.

"I was called. For two years I tried every conceivable way to effect the release of the usurper from the body of the child without success. The case became an obsession with me. I sold my practice in Vienna.

"At first I set up a practice in Chicago, and kept an office there. Then finally I gave even that up. With the consent of the parents I moved into the house, and I have been here since then, devoting what little skill I have to the problem."

The doctor's shoulders sagged in dejection. "If I had been called while the girl was still in possession of her reason I might have succeeded. If the girl had learned to love me as I—" He stopped abruptly.

"You love this girl?" I asked.

"Yes." He nodded his head sadly. "Why do you think I gave up my practice? My future?"

HIS face became stern. "Yes I love her. And equally I hate the soul of her sister; the sister whose dead body lay twined about her while the spirit and poisons from its decaying flesh tainted the living."

Dr. Blech stood stiffly, his fists clenched, his dark, foreign face grimly fixed in lines of hate. Numbly my mind compared the flash of angry light in his eyes with the sharp, sudden glare of lightning, which lit up the window at his back to the right of the fireplace.

The century old cottage with its thick, stone walls, the leaded glass windows, the massive fireplace, and the raging storm that beat against us from outside, held back as many other storms had been held in the past hundred and fifty years, was a fitting setting for the unfolding of his tale.

As I sat there watching him, my head throbbing violently, a cigarette dangling from my nerveless lips, I would not have been surprised if his form had suddenly become indistinct, its lines changing in a blur of flowing motion, and he had dropped to all fours, a werewolf.

And slowly the meaning of what he had said began to penetrate. The girl I loved, the girl whose touch had sent electric, magic life and hope into my soul, was an upstart! An obsessing spirit! Slowly, with cold deliberation, she was driving her twin insane, trying to drive her from the body, which was rightfully hers.

The memory of the other—that helpless, sick girl in the rain whose lips had sought mine, taking what happiness she could while she had the chance; and the memory of those eyes as they held mine in magic embrace in the Old Heidelberg, while the spirit in them whispered, "I love you," fought in my memory.

"No!" I exclaimed aloud. My cry seemed a thing separate from me. I heard the anguish, the protest in it. "You're wrong!"

"Unfortunately I am right," the doctor said quietly.

I started to speak. He held up his hand to stop my rush of words and went on.

"You see," he said, "neither girl is aware of the existence of the other. Just as you, and every person, has a censor, which blocks off from the conscious mind all thoughts which it could not accept, and sometimes brings them through in symbological form by means of dreams, so each of these personalities, from earliest infancy onward, has built up a censor, which automatically rationalizes the inconsistencies that inevitably develop each day.

"Unlike most cases of split personality, both personalities have the same name. Both are Carolyn Andrews. Both are the only child of the Andrews. Where their memories are consistent and their desires coincide, they may be said to be one person. Where their interests and hopes clash, they are separate.

"The Carolyn you saw at the Old Heidelberg is a wonderful girl. She does not know that in her subconscious she is deliberately plotting the overthrow and eviction of her sister from the body she herself has no right to. If she could be told the truth she would be horrified and perhaps not believe it. For reasons I'll explain later, you must meet her and get acquainted with her. For the same reasons you must meet her sister under—ah, more favorable circumstances than those of tonight."

DOCTOR BLECH glanced at his wristwatch. Outside the storm was abating, and the dim light of dawn was perceptible through the windows.

"Right now we both need some rest," he concluded. "This afternoon would be a good time for you to meet the girl of the Old Heidelberg formally. When you do, let nothing of all this pass your lips. Later I want to talk to you privately again. And in a few days I will convince you of the truth of all my assertions that seem so incredible now. Good night." With that he left.

I stood up and went to the window and gazed at the back of the doctor as he went along the path to the house. Was he right? He gave the impression of being a trifle abnormal himself. I realized I would have to discount this impression, because all foreigners seem a trifle abnormal. Especially so if they are Europeans who dabble in psychoanalysis and the occult.

But he confessed a love for one of the personalities resident in the girl whose name I now knew to be Carolyn Andrews. Carolyn! I had often wondered what the name would be that I would someday associate the answers to all my dreams with. And now that my dreams were being answered they were turning out to be nightmares.

77

I thought of my first attraction for this place. The hope that a lot of good ideas would come from living here that would result in stories. Stories! My livelihood. My source of income.

Suddenly the game of hatching plots and building them into interesting tales for public consumption seemed silly; the game of adolescent minds that had never experienced anything real, written for the escape of stupid, dull readers from their own uninteresting lives.

Here, and within the walls of that sinister heap of masonry, which had just swallowed the doctor, was realism, the goal of all authors—a goal that can only be attained by reality. And I was part of it. I, a dealer in cellophane wrappers in assorted tints, in which the public could wrap itself and imagine itself in a universe apart from reality. I, a seller of prosaic pipe dreams designed to lift the tired city dweller out of his cockroach infested sleeping room and transport him to the future, to other worlds, or to the adventure laden past. I had been sold a bill of goods that was genuine!

IT WAS mid-afternoon when the wall phone rang and the careful, European voice of Dr. Blech announced that my presence was requested in the drawing room of the house. His voice over the phone carried no hint of anything out of the ordinary.

I had been ready for this call for hours. Putting my Bing Crosby jacket on over my sport shirt and making sure the collar of the shirt was outside the coat where it belonged, I left the cottage and strolled casually up the path to the front door of the big stone mansion.

The doctor met me there and conducted me through a large front room, and through a massive, cream-enameled door into a room whose outer wall was taken up mostly by French doors opening onto a terrace. I had missed it before because it was on the driveway side of the house. A Hammond organ was setting in a central position, placed so that whoever played it could look out through the French doors at a somewhat uninspiring landscape of roses, Cannas, and bushes, surrounded by more of the flat, half dead lawn that I firmly believed to be as old as the house itself.

Mrs. Andrews was seated stiffly erect on a backless walnut seat. Standing near her was Carolyn. *My* Carolyn, as I now referred to her in my thoughts.

She was dressed as she had been at the Old Heidelberg, minus the hat. Her blond hair showed no signs of the soaking it had had the night before, and was done up in the casual way some girls can affect and make it look like it had just come from the beauty shop.

As I came through the door her expression was that of idle curiosity blended with interest. I guessed she had been told the new gatekeeper was a young man who wrote stories for a living and had applied for the job because of the housing shortage. At least the look on her face seemed to indicate that.

Then she recognized me. I saw the startled look come into her eyes, and sensed the wheels start to go around in her pretty head. A slow flush crept up from her neck and spread over her face.

Suddenly I knew what she was thinking. She thought that I had in some way known who she was and had taken the job in order to meet her!

"Carolyn, this is Jack Marley," Dr. Blech had said. She seemed not to have heard. Anger at the daring she thought I had had in taking a job just to meet her, undisguised pleasure at the knowledge I had, embarrassment, forgiveness for my supposed daring, pleasure again, and embarrassment again, rushed to her face in rapid succession.

Then she woke up to the fact that Dr. Blech had said something, did a rapid double take and landed gracefully on her feet, mentally—the casual, well bred young lady meeting a social freak.

"HOW do you do, Mr.— I don't believe I quite got the name?" It was the first I had heard her voice. I liked the way her lips moved when she talked, and there was a resonant quality to her voice that goes vaguely by the name dusky.

"Jack Marley," Dr. Blech repeated.

She held out her hand, an impish smile on her lips. Remembering the shock of touching her in the restaurant I hesitated. Then I put mine in hers. It was cool and pleasant. I left it there as long as I dared, drinking the heady draft of her blue-green, twinkling eyes. She had recovered her sense of humor and I matched her mood with relief. There would be time enough later to convince her that I had not known she lived here when I took the job. Or should I tell her?

I don't know what we talked about. Somehow without being aware of saying anything, we found out that we both enjoyed swimming, that she had read something of mine under a pen name and thought it wonderful, that the electric organ was hers and that she played it quite well.

Then we discovered that we were alone.

"How rude of mother and Henry to leave without being excused," Carolyn exclaimed merrily to cover her embarrassment at the realization that she had betrayed her interest in me so easily.

I didn't want to come out of the clouds, so I suggested something on the organ. She played several things I didn't know, but which were really something. I suggested that I could play a little, more to get a chance to sit beside her than to exhibit my skill or lack of it.

I sat down and played a few tunes by ear, switched to Rachmaninoff, my only serious achievement, and then we wound up in a dual with Chopsticks.

I don't know how it happened. We were laughingly slaughtering Chopsticks when our hands got tangled up. Suddenly I was holding hers and we were close together. She looked up at me, a dreamy, half-frightened look in her eyes. Then slowly I kissed her.

With her lips against mine and the ancient walls benignly looking on, I thought, "If I lose you after having found you life won't be worth living."

THEN she drew away from me and sat leaning back slightly, a half-wondering amazement in her eyes. I knew there was a smile on my lips. But that's all I really knew.

Then I held out my arms and she came into them. I sensed the relief with which she accepted the fact of loving me. By some strange alchemy of love the mystery and problems that were walled up in her subconscious became mine. And I *knew* that here was no upstart obsessor. I *knew* the doctor was wrong.

Finally Carolyn raised her head from where it had lain on my shoulder. There was a shyness in the look she gave me. Unconsciously her hand raised to straighten out her hair and she gave an embarrassed chuckle.

"Well, what do we do now?" she asked.

I took her face in my hands and gave her a tender kiss, and said, "We act very prosaic and pretend we just like each other in a polite way so as to convince the doctor and your mother that we think we are fooling them, when they have undoubtedly been peeking through the keyhole for the last half hour—and know what has been going on whether they have been peeking or not."

This appealed to her, so we strode casually into the other room, her fingers twined in mine, and we both strived with only a little success to attain the appearance of careless friendliness, enjoying the transparent fraud of our little game.

Carolyn's mother and Dr. Blech, pretending to be quite interested in something in the newspaper, co-operated quite well with us in our mutual deception.

I watched the doctor curiously, trying to detect signs of jealousy. Although the Carolyn I loved, and who loved me, was not the one *he* loved, the lips I had kissed, the living, vibrant body I had held in my arms, were those that he too, longed to hold.

Perhaps he had already, when the other Carolyn was dominant. The jealousy I had looked for in him suddenly welled up in me. And with it a knowledge that come what may, I would fight to the last ditch, and by any means, fair or foul, to get rid of the other Carolyn and take my Carolyn away from this place.

While all this was going on in the back of my mind, the four of us were making serious attempts to carry on a casual, friendly conversation. Now I threw myself into it with a will, and was soon my ordinary self.

The conversation got around to story writing. The inevitable question, "Where do you get your ideas?" came from Carolyn herself.

"It's like an equation in mathematics," I said. I had gone over all this many, many times, so did not have to think too much of what I was saying.

"You have a perfectly ordinary series of events in real life. It's like a single specific solution to mathematical equation. Let all the answers become variables. Let some of them vary one way, others vary another. The result is something that might take place in real life, but somehow never does. Therefore it becomes interesting fiction.

"For example," I warmed up to my subject. "You hear of people having nervous breakdowns over troubles, and even going nuts in the face of some insoluble dilemma. You have scientists spending their lives trying to unravel the mysteries of the past of the human race. You hear of hair turning white overnight because of some trying event. You read of Freud and his psychoanalysis restoring the sanity of people by finding out what drove them insane. You see, in your mind's eye, the friends and relatives of these insane people taking them to the psychiatrist so that he can find the clue to their madness.

"Put them all into a variable setup. Let some people go mad. Let the mystery be—not in their mental makeup, but hidden in a series of events. This series of events will make up the body of the story when it is written. Cut out the psychiatrist and let the reader take his place. Let the writer be the friend who is taking the case to the reader, with his friends the innocent victims. What have you really got?

"You have a mystery hidden in a perfectly ordinary, or maybe not so ordinary, series of events. The mystery is penetrated by your friends, who promptly go mad. Push that to the extreme and have them become mindless creatures who can't take care of themselves. You, the writer, are taking the case before the reader because you can't solve the mystery yourself. If the reader, after reading what happened can penetrate the mystery and doesn't himself go mad, maybe he can supply the clue to the restoring of your friends to their normal state."

CAROLYN and her mother laughed delightedly at the picture I had built up. Dr. Blech chuckled politely, but the frown on his face indicated that he was wondering where I was headed.

"Now," I went on, "you have the framework of a fascinating story. All you have to do is conjure up a series of events that will fit into the framework without letting the reader down in his expectations after reading the buildup. I actually wrote such a story. I made the mystery be some mysterious entity, which I left as either the mass consciousness of humanity or as some last man, alone on the planet in the future after the rest of the race has died out, probing into the past in an effort to change what happened. In the background I built up the mystery quite definitely, but never brought it all out, because the mystery the way it stood offered the reader a chance to solve it. No doubt when it is printed someone might *really* solve something and actually go mad. Then I'll become a second Orson Welles!"

Now even the doctor laughed. I wasn't through with the subject yet, but I didn't know whether I dared go on. I decided to risk it.

"The series of events in the story I wrote was designed for a specific public; the readers of a fantasy magazine. But the same skeleton could have any number of 'series of events' as its foundation. Instead of suddenly going mad, the victims could spend years at it, while they lived in the midst of the mystery, unable to solve it. They might even think they have solved it and not be able to do anything to end it. They might not know they have *gone* mad. They might be mistaken in their solution to the mystery."

"You see," I concluded, "with that one plot a thousand stories can be written. You can have one, four, or any number of people go mad, in any number of ways. You can have a hero solve the mystery, you can leave it for the reader, you can set the story in a scientific laboratory, a home, on a ship at sea, on an island, or even in the African jungle."

"Do all your stories follow this plot?" Mrs. Andrews asked.

"No. Heaven forbid!" I exclaimed. "Writers who stick to one plot become monotonous. They might keep the same characters as is done in lots of the most popular detective fiction, but the plots must vary. Otherwise the writer's reading public soon shies away from him."

The big double doors on one side of the room emitted rattling noises, then opened wide, pushed from the other side by a tall, English looking butler.

Dinner was obviously ready. I arose in haste, ready to make hasty excuses and leave. I had suddenly remembered that I was only the gatekeeper, and that I was supposed to eat with the servants.

Mrs. Andrews read my mind and said, "You will have dinner with us, of course, Mr. Marley. And now that we know you, you may forget all about being gatekeeper. Goodness knows we never have need of one. I think I keep one on only because I hate to have the cottage unoccupied." She laughed gaily. "After hearing how you write a story I could never regard you as one of my servants again."

"Thank you," I said. Carolyn took my hand and led me into the dining room.

DURING dinner I thought it was the most enjoyable meal I had ever had. Carolyn sat across from me, and we carried on a conversation with our eyes that was just between us, while at the same time keeping up our end of the general conversation.

The doctor had become quite human. I began to like him.

Toward the end of the meal I noticed that Carolyn began to look a little tired. Then, when we finally rose from the table, she said, "I feel awfully like a baby, Jack, but will you excuse me? I feel too sleepy to remain awake. Perhaps after a little nap I'll feel better."

"Of course," I said hastily.

"Of course," the doctor echoed. "If you do not wake up in time to see him again this evening he will be here tomorrow."

"That's right," she smiled. She looked back and gave me a parting, tender smile as she went through the door. After she had gone I thanked Mrs. Andrews for the dinner and started to excuse myself.

"Wait," the doctor said. "In a few moments you will meet the other Carolyn. When you have been here longer you will learn to recognize the symptoms of transition."

Mrs. Andrews smiled sadly and said nothing. We were in the front room now, so I sat down on one of the high backed antiques and said nothing. Dr. Blech picked up the evening paper and looked at it without reading anything. Mrs. Andrews just sat there. I doubt if she was even thinking.

I could understand her better now. The blankness of mind that I had sensed in her at our first meeting I saw now to be a wall of reserve. In what I considered to be the evening of life, at fifty-three, when most people have all their big events behind them and look forward to a life of relaxation and uneventful years, she had suddenly been visited by tragedy and had had to live with it since.

She had walled in her feelings, cultivated a calm exterior for so long that it had become an automatic mask, impenetrable to the casual onlooker.

She noticed I was studying her and gave me a friendly smile. I returned it.

The door opened and Carolyn returned. She didn't seem to notice me at first, coming in with an air of careless let down, not bothering to notice anyone in the room.

"I feel so listless," she said in a petulant voice. "I always feel so let down after a storm."

Her roving eyes settled on me. "Oh, hello," she exclaimed. "Aren't you the young man who rescued me from myself in the rain last night? It was so nice of you to do that. And it was so mean of the doctor to hit you over the head." She tittered, putting her hand over her mouth.

I looked sharply at the doctor. He looked embarrassed and said lamely, "I didn't know quite what to do. I did the first thing that came to mind."

"He is so funny," the new Carolyn said. "He is foreign, you know. And he's in love with me. I think it was jealousy that made him hit you over the head. He picked me up and carried me back to the house and left you laying there in the rain. And in your pajamas, too." She laughed gleefully. Then concern appeared on her face. "I hope you didn't catch cold. Did you? But I didn't kiss Henry when he carried me to the house," she went on without waiting for an answer to her question. "His kisses are so tragic. I suppose that is his idea of emotion. But your kisses are terrific. They are so alive. And it was so thrilling to have you appear out of the storm and sweep me off my feet in such a stormy fashion. I never had that happen before in my life. You know, I think someone told me you are the new gatekeeper. Won't you tell me about yourself? But I suppose you are married and your wife is here with you. That is the way it always is.

"Oh, you aren't!" she exclaimed. "Oh, that's *so* nice."

I HAD listened to this verbal tirade with increasingly mixed up feelings. A horrible, sickening feeling was growing in the pit of my stomach, and I could feel the food that I had eaten with such pleasure knot up in my stomach.

I looked at the doctor helplessly. He looked his encouragement, but it didn't help. Then he tried to put things on a more conventional basis.

"This is Jack Marley, the new gatekeeper," he said. "He writes stories and took the position because of the housing shortage."

"Oh, how simply romantic," she exclaimed, holding out her hand. I took it. It was still cool to the touch. As I held it there, imprisoned against its will this time, a thousand thoughts rushed into my brain. A plea for help, for understanding, for trust and confidence, seemed to flow secretly from the hand into my brain, from the sleeping Carolyn whose subconscious knew what was going on.

The Carolyn of the storm asked breathlessly for me to tell her about story-writing. Reluctantly I repeated much of what I had said earlier, each word seeming to become desecrated as it left my lips for the ears of this mad, prattling creature that looked out of Carolyn's eyes.

I wanted to excuse myself and rush out of the house and walk and walk and walk, until the exertion had erased the taint of this experience from my mind. I wanted to, but I dared do nothing except sit there and be nice, because I could not know what harm I might do by any other course.

I wanted to switch the subject but my brain was too numb to make the effort. It was a welcome relief when her shallow mind lost interest in my account and seized on a new train of thought of her own.

I had been telling mechanically of the build-up of a plot. She broke in.

"That's so interesting. I was in a hospital once. Mother has always been ill and had to have a doctor. That is why Henry lives here. He's a doctor, you know. Mother was very ill so the doctor we had before Henry took me out to his sanitarium to stay for a few months. It was so interesting."

She broke off and went to the window. It had grown dark outside. The storm of the night before had gone, and most of the rain had now soaked into the ground. She turned and looked pleadingly into my eyes.

"The night is so beautiful. I always love it. Would you like to walk with me on the grounds? It is so beautiful out there."

I looked appealingly at Dr. Blech. He nodded sternly. It was a command. I saw the hurt in his eyes. The grim self-control. In that moment I pitied him more than I did this frail, senseless spirit that dwelt in Carolyn. I saw the life he was wasting. His own life, so full of promise eleven years ago when he was a world-renowned psychiatrist.

I completed in my mind the plot I had hinted at in my conversation. The two Carolyns were the series of events. The century-and-a-half-old mansion with its cold stone walls was the setting. And the one slowly going mad because he could not resolve the mystery was the doctor. Perhaps Mrs. Andrews was already mad. Perhaps her cloak of conventional niceties hid a mind that had lost its reason long ago. Perhaps my feeling about her the first time I saw her was correct. Perhaps her spirit *had* departed, years ago, unnoticed.

It wasn't a mystery for the reader to thrill over and try to solve, and go mad himself so that I could become a second Orson Welles. It was a mystery that might very well leave me a mindless creature, but of which I was now an integral part. I would have to resolve it or go mad myself.

But what could *I* do? A writer with a casual knowledge of many subjects, but master of none? Could I be right when a world-renowned expert was sure *he* was right? And if he *was* right, assuming that he could eventually drive one of these two Carolyns away forever, would it be right to banish the sane, lovable Carolyn—*my* Carolyn, into the darkness of disembodiment or oblivion so that this witless, prattling creature, that was now making my ears crawl with her senseless conversation, could remain permanently?

MY MIND was jerked back to my surroundings as Carolyn took my arm and firmly directed me toward the door. We were out, wandering along the border of the flowerbeds. Vaguely I was aware that her voice had become quiet and intimate.

It kept on without interruption. It asked questions without waiting for an answer. It switched without warning from one subject to another, often doing so in the middle of a word even, leaving the old subject dangling.

She walked close to me, her hair brushing my shoulder. The spell of the night before returned. The realization that this was the body of *my* Carolyn was strong in my mind. By blotting out the endless prattle, consigning it to the gloom that softly hid the dying lawn, making it no different than a young, green carpet of tender shoots under my feet; by imagining that it was really *my* Carolyn's hair that the gentle breeze tossed playfully against my neck, I could almost imagine the rest to be a nightmare of my professional imagination, and that it didn't really exist.

We had stopped under a tree. Her voice had become a soothing, meaningless, hypnotic sound. Then she was against me, yielding, feminine, and my arms went around her.

Her face lifted, a white oval in the dark, with its blue-green eyes beckoning. Her lips found mine, hungrily. The madness of the storm returned. In my mind the thunders crashed and the lightnings flashed across the sky. I felt the beat of her heart against mine, the quickness of her breath, the trembling of her body.

Then a nausea and an overwhelming disgust hit me. I crushed her angrily and then released her. She fell, sobbing, to lay at my feet.

I looked at her huddled figure silently for a moment, sick with indecision and self-disgust. Then I turned and went to my cottage. As I went I was aware of the figure of the doctor as it left the shadow of a tree and went toward the pitiful creature I had left.

I knew what I was going to do. My mind was made up. I went to the bedroom and started throwing sox, shirts, and things in my suitcase. I started putting books back in the boxes I had taken them out of that morning.

In my heart I knew that my love for the *real* Carolyn would bring me back. But I was going. Things broke as I slammed them into boxes. I cursed monotonously as things resisted my efforts to put them away in their packing cases.

I stood up and lit a cigarette with trembling fingers. The doctor was standing quietly in the doorway.

Glaring at him, I returned to my work of packing. He said nothing.

"You are quitting?" he asked finally.

There was a carefulness in his voice like the carefulness with which you talk to a crazed killer with a gun, or like the carefulness with which you handle a rattlesnake.

Through some quirk of male psychology this flattered me. My anger abated. I grew angry at the weakening of my anger.

"Yes," I said. "I'm getting out of this madhouse. *You* are insane yourself, doctor. Do you know that? Giving up a practice and a life dedicated to society to lose yourself in a hopeless love for a mad, obsessing spirit. *I'm* not going to do the same. I'm getting out while there is still time. If I don't I'll never be able to write another story again."

"DO YOU think you can leave all this just by going?" Dr. Blech asked in the same careful voice. "I have studied you carefully. I don't think you can forget your love for the other Carolyn or her love for you. That love that made you hurt *my* Carolyn. That love has kept *me* here, and driven me insane, as you say."

His voice became tragically bitter. "I couldn't leave if I tried. I have tried, without success.

"Do you think I am going to *let* you leave?" he continued, his voice taking on an angry, desperate note. "I've waited at least eight years for you to come. I'm not going to let you go now."

"What do you mean?" I asked, bewildered.

"I mean simply this," he answered. "I am going to prove to you that the girl you crushed and left lying on the lawn is the rightful possessor of that body. I'm going to convince you that you have it in your power to give that body to her and her alone, ending this tragedy. It will hurt. I know how it will hurt you. Haven't I suffered myself as much as any human can suffer?"

"Just how are you going to prove all this?" I asked belligerently.

"When I carried Carolyn into the house I put her into a state of hypnotic trance to wipe out the effects of your stupid actions. She is still in that state. Come with me and I'll prove what I say."

I followed the doctor, wonderingly. He continued his explanation as we went to the house.

"In the hypnotic state the subconscious mind of each personality can be called up and questioned," he said in a hushed voice. "By questioning it we can establish its identity as belonging to one or the other of the personalities. Then we can ask it anything we wish and it will answer, because it is subject completely to my will after I have hypnotized the patient."

He was now the doctor, sure and confident of himself. I quickened my steps. He led me upstairs and into a room, which I saw at once to be his office, his link with the past when he had been in practice.

Carolyn was lying on a tilted metal chair of a type I had seen in doctors' offices, which can be either a chair or an operating table. She was unconscious, her face lit up by a spotlight above her head—the only light in the room.

"She is asleep," the doctor whispered. "I have learned how to call either personality into wakefulness at will."

"Then why can't you order one to remain unconscious permanently and end this dual state of affairs?" I asked.

"Because," the doctor whispered, "there is some physiological factor connected with fatigue that controls that ordinarily, and post-hypnotic suggestion seems to have no effect on that whatever."

"Oh," I whispered.

"Just watch now," the doctor requested. "Don't say anything." He stroked the forehead of the sleeping girl soothingly for a moment.

Then he said in a quiet, droning voice, "I want to talk to Caroline. Will you answer, Caroline?"

The lips moved slowly. "Yes," came the answer.

"What happened today, Caroline?" the doctor asked. My eyes were fixed on her lips. They moved as if the spirit within could barely reach them.

"What—do—you—mean?" she asked.

"Did you play the organ?" the doctor suggested.

The face, unearthly looking in the eerie light, smiled happily. "Yes. I played chopsticks with— I love him. He's— He's—"

THE doctor's expression became grim as he framed his next question. He spoke slowly, "Is this body you are in your own?"

Carolyn's face became puzzled. "I—don't—know," she replied. "I—seem to remember—dying and yet I wasn't dead. I crawled in with my—sister. But I have no sister."

"Can you leave her and go away?" asked the doctor.

She remained silent.

"Would you leave if I ordered you to leave," Dr. Blech asked.

"No," she said simply.

"Carolinn," the doctor called softly, accenting the difference in pronunciation.

The face changed. No line of it seemed to move, yet the retreat of the spirit of Caroline and the presence of Carolinn could be seen under the white, unnatural light of the lamp. I felt cold beads of perspiration on my forehead. I was witnessing something that could not be in reality.

The doctor remained quiet, watching. At last he asked, "What did you do today, Carolinn?"

"I don't know what you mean," came the reply.

"Did you play the organ?" asked Dr. Blech.

"The organ?" she echoed. "No, I didn't play the organ. I—I—" She became silent.

"Is this your rightful body that you are in?"

"Yes," came the firm reply. Then, in a helpless voice, "But my sister is driving me away and I don't want to go away." A puzzled look came slowly to her face. "But I *have* no sister."

"Can't you drive her away?" asked the doctor.

"She won't let me," she answered slowly. "She—keeps—me—out."

Dr. Blech looked at me significantly. "Are you convinced now?" he asked bitterly.

"No!" My voice was hoarse with emotion. I looked at the doctor's dark, European face, the lights and shadows painted on it by the single light, the glinting dark eyes, as it crouched over the unconscious body of Carolyn—*my* Carolyn.

A thousand thoughts were rushing through my mind. Memories of things I had read in books on hypnotism, psychology, abnormal psychology, and in stories. Things began to fit together. Unrelated things. Something in an old book on mesmerism clicked with something in a book on spiritualism.

"Would it be possible," I asked quietly, "for me to ask questions of Caroline while she is hypnotized?"

"I don't know," the doctor answered. "I could order her to answer your questions and see."

"Do that," I said.

Dr. Blech called Caroline back. I watched the portrayal of the transition of personality on her face.

Finally, when the struggle of transition was over, he gave his order.

"Can you hear me, Caroline?" I asked.

"Yes, Jack. I can hear you," she answered.

So far so good. I glanced at the doctor. He had stood back, his face inscrutable. I stared into the motionless eyes of the girl, which were fixed unmoving on the overhead light. I tried to force my thoughts and will past them to the spirit that lay quiescent behind them.

Then, slowly I asked my question. "Is it your own body that you are in, or your sister's?"

THE doctor's eyes flashed at me, but I held my attention concentrated on Carolyn, waiting for the answer. Finally it came.

"Yes, Jack, it is my body."

I heard the doctor's startled gasp, and looked at him triumphantly. He opened his mouth to say something but I motioned him to silence. I was not through.

"Do you love me, Caroline?" I asked.

"Yes." The answer came faintly.

"If I helped, could you drive your sister away so that—?"

With a startled oath the doctor leaped around the table. His sudden attack caught me by surprise. I was borne back. I felt myself falling. I clutched at the doctor, his maniacal face a mask of insane frenzy above me.

My clutching fingers met only empty air. My head struck something hard and sharp. I didn't quite lose consciousness. Dimly I was aware of the doctor standing over me, his breath harsh, his face and figure nightmarish in the room's single light.

I saw him go to a cabinet and come back with a roll of adhesive tape. My mind strained to make my muscles obey its will, without success. Then I knew no more.

Consciousness returned slowly. For what seemed like hours I was aware only of a dull beating. I thought at first it must be waves from the ocean beating against the shore. Then an undertone of pain began to accompany each pounding wash of the waves.

I studied this new sensation in a detached way for another hour or two, so it seemed. Then I went to sleep. I awoke with a start that made the pounding begin again. This time it was in my head. But also I could feel. I was lying on something hard and cold. It was dark. I tried to move my hands, but they seemed paralyzed.

I remembered what had happened then, and wondered without surprise if I were dead. The cool, detached way I was thinking made it seem quite plausible that I might be dead.

"I hope, if I *am* dead, that Dr. Blech can drive Caroline out of her body so that she can be with me," I thought absently.

The memory of Dr. Blech made me sit up. A wave of dizziness made me fall back, but the simple act of sitting up had shown me I was still alive. I rolled over and felt the floor with my face. It was made of stone. I must be in some sub-cellar of the house.

The cool stone floor against my cheek revived me a little. I began to think.

What could the doctor possibly gain by putting me down here? When he released me he would be liable to assault, kidnapping, and many other things, not to mention malpractice. He would probably land in a mental hospital before it was over.

But maybe he didn't ever intend for me to be set free! The thought—the inescapable logic of it, made sweat stand out all over me! Then why hadn't he killed me outright?

Maybe he wanted to keep me alive for some mad experiment. Maybe he wanted to gloat while he taunted me. Maybe he still thought I could be of use to him in ridding Carolyn's body of Caroline. *My Carolyn.* I ground my teeth in impotent frustration.

Out of the darkness a throaty chuckle sounded. My hair rose on my scalp.

"I see that you have regained consciousness," the doctor's voice spoke. "I must have dozed while I was waiting."

His lighter flared as he lit a cigarette. It illumined his face, and I thought of Old World creatures of legend as I looked at it fascinatedly. When he put his lighter away the flame of the cigarette as he puffed deeply on it still cast an eerie light over his countenance, making it a mask of evil cunning and insane hate.

His voice was calm and self-assured as he went on.

"I will have to kill you after a while," he said regretfully. "But only if I succeed in what I am going to do. I've thought about it for a long time. You see, there is *one* way in which I can drive the spirit of Caroline from the body and leave only the spirit of my Carolinn.

"I want to explain it to you," he went on. "The native spirit of the body is more firmly entrenched than the obsessor. If I could get the obsessor out just once, I could keep it out permanently by means of static electricity, which is known to confuse it.

"At death the obsessor would leave the body first, since it is the more loosely connected. So, for an instant after death, the native spirit would be left in sole possession of the body."

I tried to speak, but my mouth was sealed with tape. Dr. Blech ignored my mumbled sounds and went on.

"Death can be produced instantly and without harm to the body tissues by means of electric shock," he said calmly. "Sometimes the dead person so killed can be restored to life by means of injection of adrenaline into the heart. There are cases on record of that happening."

"SEVERAL times I have tried it out on animals," he continued. "Sometimes I failed to restore life, and sometimes I was able to bring the animal back to life. I've hesitated to attempt it with Carolyn, because it was better to have her sometimes, even though she was not sane, than to lose her entirely, beyond hope of getting her back.

"But now I am faced with the necessity of trying the final experiment," he said sadly. "I must kill my love in order that she might live. And after I have done that I must kill you. If I don't succeed I, of course, will not care to live myself, so there will be no necessity of killing you then.

"I'm sorry, Jack," he said with regret. "You see, I like you very much. But understand that I have loved Carolyn for eleven years. You have loved her only a week. Without her life would be meaningless to me. What you started to say up above—I saw that you might succeed, and I suddenly realized that I could not let you succeed. You have forced the issue."

There was a sound of a bolt sliding back. An oblong of light appeared in the wall and the floor of the basement came into view as the door swung back. The doctor stood framed in the light.

He looked back at me, and said, "If I fail, someone will find you before long. If I succeed I will be back." With that pronouncement he closed the door. I heard the bolt slide into place. Then the silence became dense.

Frantically I started to work on my wrists. At first I couldn't move them at all. The continual straining against them finally began to produce results. I could move them up and down a little.

The room became stifling as time passed. My breath came in hoarse rasping sobs as desperation and the fear of failure pressed down on me.

How long would it take him to get ready for his experiment? That question pounded at me.

My wrists were sore and numb. Perspiration crept into my eyes and caused them to smart. I was sobbing in hopeless despair when finally I felt my hands slip free.

I cursed the numbness of my fingers that prevented them from freeing my ankles. I chaffed them and gradually brought circulation back to them. After centuries my legs were freed and I stood up.

Which direction was the door? I found the wall and followed it around. I passed three corners and cursed my luck, which made me go the long way around. Then the wooden panel was under my bleeding palm. I found the bolt and slid it back.

I half ran, half crawled up the stairs to the first floor of the house. No lights were on, and I stumbled over things in the darkness. It didn't matter, my hoarse, deafening breathing would arouse everybody anyway. I *wanted* them awake.

My hands fumbled clumsily at slippery doorknobs. Finally I was climbing the stairs to the second floor. There was a light under the door of the doctor's office. I tried the knob. The door was locked.

I beat on the panel, shouting hoarsely for the doctor to open up. Other doors opened. Mrs. Andrews came into the hall, alarm and fear on her face. She found the light switch and flooded the hallway with illumination.

I BACKED up and rammed my shoulder against the door. Between breaths I tried to explain what had been going on.

The butler came down from the third floor. At once he joined my efforts to break down the heavy door.

"I've been suspecting Henry's sanity for a long time," he ground out.

Finally, with one last burst of effort, the door gave way. I stepped inside.

Carolyn was not on the operating table. The overhead light was still on, but the room was vacant.

I stood there, stunned, blankly gazing at the empty table under the light, at the sinister emptiness of the white-walled room. With a sinking sensation I saw the dozens of square miles of Chicago, with the doctor somewhere in those wide spaces, carrying out his mad scheme.

A single, despairing, "No..." sobbed past my lips.

The butler pushed past me to the phone on the desk and rapidly dialed a number. He was calling the police.

"Oh, they're on their way," he said. He hung up.

Almost immediately I heard the distant wail of a siren. The maid's voice in the doorway said that she had called the police when she heard the disturbance.

I sank exhausted into a chair, and leaned my head dejectedly on the table where Carolyn had lain under the hypnotic spell of the mad Viennese doctor a short hour or so ago.

The police came into the room. A quiet man in a tan suit took over. As briefly as I could I told him what had happened.

"Jerry," he said, "go down and see if a car is missing in the garage. Joe, get the license numbers and descriptions of all the cars so that we can broadcast the description of the one the doctor took. You, Bill," pointing at a third man, "get on that phone and see if any calls were made from this phone in the last two hours. Work on long distance. She's the only one who would have any record of calls."

I began to see a glimmering of hope. In a few minutes the description of the car the doctor had taken was being broadcast to all prowl cars. Then a number was repeated by the man at the phone. Dr. Blech had made a call.

The number was put through. I could hear the endless ringing at the other end. Finally, when I had given up hope, a voice answered. The detective spoke swiftly.

"Did Dr. Blech call you a little earlier this morning?"

A pause. Then, "This is the police. No time to explain." Another pause. "Yes." A longer pause. The detective hung up.

"Dr. Blech just left there. He got the key to the other doctor's office. It seems that there are electrical things at that office that Dr. Blech had to have for his experiment. This doctor will meet us at the building where his office is."

He looked at me sympathetically. "I suppose you want to go along," he said.

I nodded and was out of the door ahead of him. The men in the car were silent as the car sped at uncanny speed through the almost deserted streets in the early dawn.

Even at that it was almost fifteen minutes before we drew up in front of the building. A car sat at the curb. The detectives looked at it, then nodded to one another. It was the car the mad doctor had taken.

I looked up. Far up a light shone through one of the office windows. Up there Dr. Blech was performing his mad experiment. He was going to kill Carolyn, then bring her back to life! But he himself had said that probably she would not *come* back to life."

THERE was a maddening delay while a slow moving night watchman came to the door. Finally we were in, and speeding upward in an elevator. It came to a stop and the night watchman opened the door. Quickly we stepped into the hall and traversed the fifty feet of hallway to the door the light came through.

The night watchman had given up the master key and gone back down to answer the frantic buzzing of the elevator bell that had begun when we were part way up.

"Probably Dr. Graney," the detective had remarked, referring to the doctor whose office Dr. Blech was in.

With quick efficiency the detective inserted the master key in the lock and opened the door. The other men had drawn their guns. The detective flung open the door and jumped aside.

There was a second of silence while we took in the empty reception room and the details of the layout. At one side was a half-opened door. The faint hum and crackling of electric machinery came faintly to our ears.

In a few short strides I was past the police and standing in the doorway of the inner room. Carolyn lay on an operating table, motionless. Dr. Blech stood a few feet away, his hand resting on a switch on a panel of a complicated electrical device.

For a moment he looked at me, triumph, gloating, and madness written in the lines of his face. Then he plunged home the switch.

Carolyn's body gave a single, convulsive jerk as the unleashed forces from the machine seared their way through her flesh. Then the doctor pulled the switch open.

She was dead! Carolyn was dead!

The police tried to crowd past me.

"Wait," I ordered. "She is dead. If we interfere now, nothing can save her. Dr. Blech *must* be allowed to finish."

"You are right, my dear Mr. Marley," Dr. Blech said. His voice held triumph and silent amusement. He turned his eyes to a clock on the wall, his hand grasping a hypodermic syringe lying on a white table at his side. The needle was at least six inches long, and looked fragile.

I watched the seconds move by, marked by the sweep of a long second hand on the face of the clock. I didn't breathe.

Then, slowly, Dr. Blech slipped the point of the needle between two ribs and shoved it toward the heart. I watched the needle gradually grow shorter. Finally it became stationary.

Carefully, deliberately, the plunger went down, forcing the fluid in the hypodermic needle into the heart. The plunger stopped. Then the needle was withdrawn.

A faint flush appeared on the pale skin of the breast. The nostrils quivered and the chest expanded convulsively. Carolyn was alive again! But *which* Carolyn would it be?

Dr. Blech stood quietly, a faint sneer on his face, waiting.

A stranger pushed past me, his eyes taking in the details of the silent drama. He felt for Carolyn's pulse, but said nothing. Almost carelessly he pulled back her eyelid, exposing the white of the eye, and then let it drop back into place.

Dr. Blech stood motionless. He seemed not to be aware that the other doctor was there.

Dr. Graney looked at the police, and pointing to Dr. Blech, said, "Take this man into custody."

Two officers moved carefully around the operating table and took hold of Dr. Blech's arm. He moved unresisting, his eyes blank. They led him out into the reception room.

DR. GRANEY glanced hastily at Carolyn, then went to a desk phone, calling a number after dialing operator. He spoke briefly into the phone and then hung up.

"The hospital is rushing over a trained nurse," he said briskly. "Now all of you clear out. The next few hours are going to be nip and tuck. If she pulls through all right you can see her then," he said, looking at me.

"You might come back in an hour and wait in the reception room," he called after me as I went into the other room.

I didn't leave the reception room. The Chicago police force turned out to be human. They brought me up some coffee, and one of their men stayed with me.

The doctor came out and had a cup of it too, once. He drank it in silence and then went back to Carolyn, closing the door behind him.

I paced the floor. Which would it be? That question kept pounding into my brain. And there could be no answer until she opened her eyes and spoke. Which would it be?

Nine o'clock came. The regular nurse moved about the room. People came in and sat down, and read magazines. After a curious glance at me and the policeman they left us alone.

And the panel of the inner office remained silent and uncommunicative.

Finally it moved. The door swung open idly and the doctor, a white coat on now, smiled at me and said, "You can come in now."

I walked slowly through the door. Carolyn lay on a cot against the wall. Her blue-green eyes were open. A smile was on her lips.

"She's been asking for you," the doctor whispered in my ear.

Still the doubt remained. I walked fearfully toward her.

When I hesitated she motioned for me to sit beside her on the edge of the cot.

Then the low, husky voice, rich and, sweet, came from her lips. "Remember chopsticks?"

Wordlessly I nodded and took her in my arms. It was *My Carolyn! My Carolyn!*

WE WERE able to take her home that afternoon. A nurse came along, and Carolyn had to be careful for several days, but she had suffered no real ill effects from the experience she had gone through.

In a week we were able to have our first swimming date together.

"Of course," Dr. Graney had said to me when we were alone one day after Carolyn came home, "we don't know if the other personality has been definitely done away with. I don't put much stock in Dr. Blech's theory of two spirits. I stick to the simple split personality theory.

"The results are going to make medical history, though. The idea of shock as a cure for schizophrenia is not new. It is used quite regularly with very good results. But the extreme remedy, actually administering a fatal shock and then restoring life, as a cure for it—that has never been tried before.

"If Dr. Blech's sanity had not been affected he might possibly be vindicated and become the founder of a new school of psychiatry. But, unfortunately, he will never be able to resume a normal life again."

"How is he?" I asked.

The doctor shook his head. "It seemed no surprise to him that Carolyn was normal when she recovered. In fact, he still insists that his theory of two spirits is correct. He claims that the spirit of the other girl is with him now! That she went to him while Carolyn lay dead on the operating table."

The doctor shook his head again and sighed. "He was a fine man. Devoted eleven years of special study on this case. But now— He's at a private sanitarium. He spends most of his time just sitting, his eyes staring blankly at nothing."

The doctor chuckled mirthlessly. "He sounds like a man talking over the phone to his wife. All he does is say, 'Yes, dear. Yes, dear. I know, dear. Yes, dear.' That's too bad, too. At one time he was considered the foremost psychiatrist in Europe."

I'm sitting in the gatekeeper's cottage now. I'm supposed to be pounding out another story. You see, I've turned the cottage into a studio office.

The heavy oak door is open, and a soft breeze is mischievously pushing some leaves across the doorstep. Through the open doorway, as I sit at my typewriter, I can see the flat expanse of half-dead grass, as it stretches to the house. I'm going to do something about that. It *could* be a nice lawn, young and alive.

But I can't concentrate on writing a story. I just sit here and listen to the sweet, quiet strains of the electric organ. No, I don't know the tune it's playing. Some classic, or maybe it isn't a classic, since it has a nice melody. Something slow and beautiful like Ol' Man River. Only that isn't it.

And Carolyn is sitting at the organ in the music room, her fingers on the ivory keys. In a moment I will give up, and go up there to the music room myself. I'll sit down beside her and play Chopsticks. And our hands will get mixed up, and then we won't play the organ.

But doggone it. I've got to earn a living. Look at all the material I have for stories now. A mysterious, old mansion with at least one secret cellar that I know of. A moth-eaten lawn, a thick stone fence, and a sinister gatekeeper's cottage. An old lady, an English butler, and a four-car garage. And a girl with blue-green eyes for the heroine.

I've even plagiarized on a title to start the thing off with. The editor is crying for a story. I'm almost broke. And here I sit, listening to the sweet, enchanting music of the organ, staring helplessly at the blank piece of paper in my typewriter.

The only thing on it is the title, and I'll probably throw that out. Even now it's beginning to look a little corny. But it fits.

Carolyn died once. Up in that office I saw her die, and live again. Some day she'll die again, for the last time. Before then I hope we will have many, so damn many happy years that it won't really matter when the time comes.

It's a story in a million, if I could only write it! But all I've got so far is the title.

"Twice To Die"

THE END

THE MIRROR

By *William Lawrence Hamling*

It was just a plain mirror—and an old one. But it could show you the strangest things...

IT WAS a long, old-fashioned mirror, covered with the antiquity of age. It was strangely out of place in the room—bright with deft touches of the modern. But Lucy had bought it, and that was enough for John Barrows. He stood in the living room before the mirror, adjusting his tie. He was having trouble with the knot. It wouldn't slip into place. His fingers kept fumbling awkwardly.

"My wife," he mumbled. "I'm going to lose her. I love Lucy more than life itself. But I know I'm going to lose her. George Carson is taking her away! God, but I can't let that happen!"

The tie wouldn't knot. John Barrows slipped it open and started anew. His thoughts were heavy. *What shall I do? Damn this mirror! I can't focus my eyes in it. Maybe it's the silver. Lucy. Of course I haven't caught them yet, but I know! Those letters, those flowers, I don't send them! George is always dropping in... Yes, I know it's him!*

My friend. Stealing my wife! Maybe he really loves her. What's the matter with this tie? She's been talking of taking a trip. Out West someplace. Reno! She could get a divorce there... It's this crazy mirror. It keeps shimmering! I can't focus my eyes. Yes, I'm going to lose her. They're both laughing at me. If I only were sure...

Barrows tugged at the tie knot and his thoughts came aloud in a low mumble.

"I know he was here last night before I came in from New York. If only I could have seen him and Lucy together..."

The tie was folding into place now. He could see it in the mirror, even though everything was hazy and shimmering. Suddenly his hand stopped manipulating the tie. He looked into the mirror and stiffened. The haziness had vanished and he saw—

Lucy was standing there beside the small liquor table. She was smiling as she poured drinks. Her low-cut evening gown revealed creamy white patches of satin skin. She was radiantly alive. She was looking up at—George Carson!

BARROWS wheeled away from the mirror. He gazed frenziedly across the living room. At the liquor table. There was nobody standing there. No Lucy, no George Carson. Sweat broke out on John Barrows' face. He stared back into the mirror. He couldn't see himself, but he did see *them*. George was moving closer now. There was a cigarette burning in his hand. He crushed it out in an ashtray and took Lucy's hands. She stopped pouring the drinks. She turned to face George and there was a happiness glowing in her eyes. George was pulling her gently to him. His arms folded around her. His head bent—and she gave her lips willingly, lingeringly.

"Stop!" Barrows' voice cried out. He was shaking and his eyes were wild with rage. His face was inches from the mirror, staring. The scene began to shimmer, grew hazy, and then was gone. He was staring into his own haggard features. And there was a strange fear in his eyes. He turned his gaze away and shook his head. *Good God!* he thought, *Am I going mad? I did see them! I know I did! This mirror—can it be—No, I must be wrong, it's impossible—but this mirror always has been peculiar. I've noticed that shimmering before. Lucy picked it up at an auction. It is an antique alright. My God, Am I going mad? No it must be my imagination. Or an illusion—I wanted to see them together. Yes, that must be it, I was thinking so hard that I did see them, in my mind of course. But...*

Barrows turned slowly away from the mirror. He forced himself to be calm. He put out all thoughts of George Carson. He even tried humming a tune. Then he turned quickly back to the glass. He looked at himself reflected there. He smiled grimly and thought aloud.

"I was out of town Saturday. I wonder what Lucy was doing Sunday evening. Sunday evening. I wonder what—"

THE glass was hazy, almost a yellow opaqueness. There was a shimmering and John Barrows shook his head. The shimmering vanished. He was looking into a reflection of the living room. The lights were soft, only two end table lamps glowing. He could see the closet at the head of the hall. He looked at the liquor table. Two empty glasses rested there. His eyes shifted to the divan.

He began to tremble and sweat broke out anew on his face. Lucy was reclining on the divan. Her rich auburn hair was brushed back over her head onto an embroidered pillow. She was clad in a sheer negligee and there was a smile of content and happiness on her face. She was looking up. There *he* was. Moving across the room toward the divan. His features were tense and expectant. He was flushed and glowing all at the same time. Now he was sitting beside her. His hands caressed her face, her neck…Lucy was clinging to him.

"Stop! Stop!" John Barrows cried out hoarsely. He twisted away from the mirror, trembling. There was a haunted fear in his eyes. A fear of the unknown, of things beyond his ken.

"John! What is it? What's the matter?"

Lucy Barrows was leaning over the upstairs landing. She was looking down toward the living room with frightened eyes.

"John, is anything wrong?" she called out again.

John Barrows stepped slowly from the living room and into the hall. He gazed up the staircase at his wife. She was beautiful standing there. There was surprise, and sudden wonder in her eyes. Her cheeks were flushed in nervous excitement. She was like a doll in a department store fairyland. The kind you want to gather in your arms. Barrows looked at her. His face was stern, unyielding. His eyes, two glowing coals of flame. Somehow his voice remained unchanged.

"Lucy, dear, come down here a moment."

Lucy Barrows moved slowly around the landing and descended the stairway. She was more like a graceful swan making an entrance into a hushed, sacred pool. She seemed to glide down the stairs. And then she was standing before him, looking up with puzzled concern.

"I heard you cry out, John…"

"It was nothing, Lucy, I was talking to myself." He looked at her very closely and for long silent moments. Did she sense that something was wrong? He saw her glance stray beyond him to the living room and back again. It was almost as if she expected to see something there, something that had made her husband cry out. Some dark secret, finally unearthed. Yes, that was it…

It was all becoming clear in his mind now as he watched her. Yes, it was all true. He could tell. That deep concern in her eyes. Was it for him? No, it was *because* of him! She was waiting for him to accuse her of her infidelity. That's what she wanted. It would make everything so simple for a divorce. Mental cruelty!

"John!" Her voice was tense, breathless. "Are you ill? Your face…" She forced a nervous laugh. "You should see yourself in a mirror!"

Mirror. Yes, there was a mirror in the living room. An old, strange mirror. I should see myself! You should see yourself!

SUDDENLY he was trembling. Her throat It was so white and soft. He could see the pulse of blood in that slender whiteness. It would be so easy to close his hands over that throat, and tighten. But no, that would be murder. The law would make him pay for that. George Carson must pay. Yes, that was it.

"I won't be home for dinner tonight, Lucy. Do you mind?" His voice was calm, his face relaxed.

She frowned. "But I don't understand, John. Where are you going?"

"I've got to make a trip back to New York. Some business that I didn't clean up last week. I'll be back late tomorrow. You won't be lonely?"

The tenseness left her. She was the doll again, soft, warm, lovable. She smiled up at him.

"No I won't be lonely, John, but I'm sorry, you have to go again. I'll find something to do while you're away."

Of course you won't be lonely, my dear. Why should you be? Isn't this just what you hoped for, prayed for? Naturally you're sorry I have to go, and of course you'll find something to do. I wonder how long it will take you to telephone after I leave?

"I won't have to pack this time, Lucy. I won't be gone long enough. I'll hurry back as soon as I can."

She kissed him lightly on the cheek and he trembled under her touch. Then he turned away to the closet at the head of the hall. He put on his topcoat. Lucy was standing in the living room, lighting a cigarette. She smiled wistfully at him as he strode out the front door.

THE house was silent and alone in the early evening. John Barrows stood in the tall shrubbery across the street, watching it. He had been standing there for over an hour. His car was parked in a small wooded sub-division a few blocks away. Any time now George Carson should be coming along.

A light flickered on in an upstairs window. Barrows breathed a satisfied sigh. That was Lucy's room. She would be dressing up there. And soon she wouldn't be lonely. She was finding something to do.

Barrows left the shadows of the shrubbery. He glanced swiftly along the street. There was another house on the far corner, but the street was deserted. He walked swiftly across it and along the side of the house. His hand reached into his topcoat pocket. It closed over the butt of a revolver. He brushed the gun aside and dug deeper in the pocket. His hand came out with a key.

There was a small patio in the back of the house. He circled it and came to the rear entrance. He fitted the key in the lock. It turned soundlessly. Then he twisted the knob and slowly pushed the door open. Seconds later he was in the kitchen, and then he was tiptoeing through the dining room and into the hall adjoining the staircase. He moved silently.

Upstairs he could hear Lucy humming. Then he had reached the end of the hall. He paused beside the closet and looked into the living room. The end table lamps were burning. It was nice and cozy. Just right. He pulled open the closet door and slipped inside. The door closed behind him, and it was dark. He settled himself in the rear of the closet, behind the clothing. His hand found the metal in his pocket. A cold grimness closed over him. He could wait now.

Time crept by. Lucy came downstairs. He could hear her moving around the living room. He could hear her humming softly. He heard the clink of glass from the liquor table. Then he heard the front door chimes.

Lucy's footsteps were quick out in the hall. He heard the door open and Lucy say:

"Hello, darling. I thought you'd never get here!"

He heard George Carson laugh, and the door close. Then they had moved into the living room. He held his breath as he heard Lucy approach the closet.

"I'll hang up your coat, George. You'll find drinks on the table."

The closet door swung open. He could see her hands grope among the hangers. He huddled deep in the rear, tense. Then the door was shut and the darkness closed in again.

He waited there, listening. They were laughing together now. Lucy's laugh was low and mellow with happiness. George's was boisterous like an excited boy's. Music drifted in to him. The laughter stopped. He could sense Lucy in George Carson's arms, dancing across the living room rug.

Time crept on.

THE music ceased. There was silence for a moment. Then the clink of glasses echoed softly. John Barrows trembled with emotion. There was no loneliness out there. But there was a great loneliness creeping into his heart. Lucy was lost. Gone. Forever. He felt his love for her turning from a despairing ache into a cold deadly hate.

It was silent out there now. Then he heard Lucy sigh. George's voice came in a low mumble of words. Barrows heard them dimly. He knew what must be done. His hand closed over the weapon in his pocket...

Only the mirror saw the closet door open. The reflection was clear and sharp in the glass. But the mirror couldn't speak. It caught the image of the hand appearing in the doorway, clutching the revolver. The two on the divan didn't see it. They weren't watching the closet. They had no reason to. But they did hear the laugh that suddenly echoed through the room. And they jumped guiltily from the divan. They stared in shocked dismay as the closet door opened fully to reveal John Barrows standing there with the gun in his hand.

Lucy screamed. George Carson stood petrified.

And the shots rang out.

They died on their feet. And their dead bodies fell limply to the floor. The shots had been sure, accurate. Straight to their hearts. The laugh came again. Cold, grim, frenzied laughter. And then there was silence...

Barrows stood looking down at them, still and quiet in death. There was no remorse in his heart, no sadness. They lay there like two castaway dolls, stripped of the beauty that had filled them in life.

Barrows took a handkerchief from his pocket and methodically wiped off the gun. He made sure his fingerprints were erased from the weapon. Then he knelt beside George Carson's body. He placed the gun in the dead man's hand, turning the limp fingers so the weapon pointed toward George Carson's heart.

Barrows rose and crossed to the liquor table. He took a long pull from an open bottle. He lighted a cigarette and surveyed the room. It was perfect. He could not have planned it better.

"You won't be lonely any longer, Lucy. Not any longer." His voice haunted the room. The stillness of death was in the air.

Barrows turned abruptly and strode off down the hall, through the dining room, into the kitchen, and out the back door. He locked it behind him.

He sat in his car for an hour. Then he started the motor and drove home, parking in front of the house. He entered the front door, closed it, and walked over to the telephone in the hall.

"Give me police headquarters, please." He caught his reflection in the mirror as he talked, and a grim smile pulled back the corners of his mouth.

IT was a clear case of suicide. The Medical Examiner said so. The police technicians examined the position of the bodies, the gun held tightly in the dead man's hand, and they agreed. They shook their heads sadly as they carted the bodies past the distraught husband standing across the living room.

Presently only Detective Charles Riley remained. He was a short redheaded Irishman, dressed in a conservative blue worsted. He was looking steadily at John Barrows.

"You loved your wife, Mr. Barrows?"

Barrows began pacing the living room rug. He turned, and agony shone in his eyes.

"I loved her more than anything in the world!"

Riley nodded. "You were aware of the affair going on between your wife and George Carson?"

Barrows' voice was sad. "Lucy loved me. I know that. George must have seen how hopeless it was for him and in a moment of frenzy decided to end his life—and Lucy's too."

The Detective walked over to the liquor table. He looked down at the open bottle of brandy. "Do you mind?" he asked.

John Barrows shook his head and continued to pace the floor. Riley poured himself a drink and sipped it slowly.

"It seems funny to me that a man who is in love with a woman would kill her and then himself."

Barrows stopped his pacing and faced the Detective with tear-stained eyes. "What do you mean?" he demanded.

Riley shrugged. "Usually in cases like this it's the third party that gets killed. It's usually done so it will look like a suicide. Then the other two can collect the insurance and marry. Provided they aren't caught in their own trap."

Barrows wrung his hands in a beautiful gesture of agony.

"Must you go on like this? Haven't I suffered enough already? If only I hadn't left her tonight—if I could have been here when that rat came! God! Lucy—I'll never forgive myself!"

Riley sighed and put down his glass. He faced John Barrows. "Well, there's no need for me to stay any longer. Of course, there'll be an inquest and you'll have to come. But it will only be a formality. The suicide verdict is almost a certainty."

Barrows breathed easier. He was calm now. He even managed a wan smile. "Of course, I understand about the inquest. I'll get your coat."

RILEY turned away from the liquor table as John Barrows walked across the room to the hall closet. Riley caught his reflection in the mirror. He approached it and straightened his tie against his collar. He looked puzzledly into the glass. It seemed to shimmer. Must be the light he decided. He couldn't get the idea out of his head that there was something queer about that suicide. It was too perfect, all too natural a setup. His thoughts mumbled aloud.

"I'd give a lot to know what actually happened here tonight."

The glass *was* shimmering. Riley frowned as he looked into it. A hazy yellow opaqueness glistened on the glassy surface. Then it was gone.

Riley stared into the mirror, transfixed. He saw the closet door opening. A hand came through that opening grasping a revolver. John Barrows stood with a gun pointing from the shadows, his face a reflected mask of hatred in the mirror.

Riley acted instinctively. His right hand dropped to his hip pocket and came up holding a gun. He jumped backward, smashing into the mirror and firing as his body twisted.

The crack of the bullet and the shatter of broken glass were simultaneous. Across the room, John Barrows swayed in pained surprise. He was standing in the closet doorway, holding a coat in his hand.

The coat fell. Barrows followed it, his body making a dull thud on the floor.

Riley stared in mute astonishment at what he had done. His gun fell from his suddenly limp fingers as he tried to reason it out.

"He was trying to kill me—I saw him! Right in the mirror…"

Riley's voice faded and his eyes fell to the smashed fragments of glass on the floor. There was something strange about them. They lay there and seemed to be shimmering. Soft kaleidoscopic shimmerings. And then a pattern seemed to form from the myriad fragments. A pattern of death and murder that came out of a closet. He saw Lucy Barrows and George Carson, their faces transfixed with fear. Then he saw their bodies lying limp and lifeless on the floor.

The shimmering grew fainter. The scene changed. He saw himself standing before the mirror. He saw John Barrows holding his coat in the closet door. He saw himself twist around, firing.

He saw… Nothing.

The shimmering was gone. The mirror was gone. There were only little bits of broken glass looking vacantly up at him.

SHARE ALIKE

By Jerome Bixby and Joe E. Dean

Casting bread upon the water is fine—as long as you're not the bread!

THEY spread-eagled themselves in the lifeboat, bracing hands and feet against the gunwales.

Above them, the pitted and barnacled stern of the *S.S. Luciano*, two days out of Palermo and now headed for hell, reared up hugely into the overcast of oily black smoke that boiled from ports and superstructure. Craig had time to note that the screws were still slowly turning, and that a woman was screaming from the crazily tilted afterdeck. Then the smoke intervened—a dark pall that lowered about the lifeboat as the wind shifted, blotting out the sky, the ship.

Fire met water. One roared; the other hissed. Gouts of blazing gasoline flared through the smoke like flame demons dancing on the waves.

Groaning, shuddering, complaining with extreme bitterness, the ship plunged.

Sky and smoke became a sickening whirl, as the lifeboat tore into the churning water in a suicidal effort to follow the parent ship to the bottom. Spray flew; waves loomed, broke, fell away; the lifeboat shipped water. Craig cursed aloud, making rage a substitute for terror. Facing him, Hofmanstahal grinned sourly.

The small boat righted itself. It was still in violent motion, lurching aimlessly across a sea jagged with whitecaps; but Craig knew that the crisis was past. He lifted his face into the cold wind, pulling himself up from the water-slopping bottom of the boat until his chin rested on the gunwale.

A wide patch of brownish foam and oil-scum spread slowly from the vortex of exploding bubbles that rose from the vanished ship.

The sea quieted. A gull swooped down and lit on an orange-crate that had bobbed to the surface.

"Well," said Craig. "Well. That's that."

HOFMANSTAHAL peeled off his shirt, wrung it out over the side. The hair that matted his thick chest and peeped from his armpits had a golden sheen that was highlighted by the sun. A small cut was under his left eye, a streak of oil across his forehead.

"You were of the crew?" he asked.

"Yes."

"But not an A.B. You are too spindly for that."

"I was navigator."

Hofmanstahal chuckled, a deep sound that told of large lungs. "Do you think you can navigate us out of this, my friend?"

"I won't have to. We're in a well-traveled shipping lane. We'll be picked up soon enough."

"How soon might that be?"

"I don't know. I don't even know if we got an SOS out; it all happened so fast." Craig sighed, rolled over so that he sat with his back curved against the side of the boat. "I doubt if we did, though. The tanks right under the radio shack were the first to go. I wonder who got careless with a cigarette..."

"M'mm. So we'll eventually be picked up. And in the meantime, do we starve?"

Craig got up tiredly. "You underestimate the Merchant Marine." He sloshed to the stern of the lifeboat, threw open the food locker. They saw kegs of water, tins of biscuits and salt meat, canned juices, a first-aid kit.

"More than enough," Craig said. He turned, searched the surrounding swells. "I wonder if any other survived..."

Hofmanstahal shook his head. "I have been looking too. No others. All were sucked down with the ship."

Craig kept looking. Smoke, heaving stained water, debris, a few dying gasoline-flames—that was all.

Hofmanstahal said, "At least we shall be well fed. Did you have any close friends aboard?"

"No." Craig sat down, pushed wet hair back from his forehead, let his hands fall to his lap. "And you?"

"Me? No one. I have outlived all my friends. I content myself with being a man of the crowd. A select group of *bon vivants* for drinking and conversation…it is enough."

SITTING with a seat between them, as if each somehow wanted to be alone, the men exchanged backgrounds. By his own account, Hofmanstahal was an adventurer. No locality could hold him for long, and he seldom revisited a place he already knew. He had been secretary to a former Resident in Malaya, and concerned himself with gems in Borneo, with teak in China; a few of his paintings had been displayed in the *Galerie des Arts* in Paris. He had been en route to Damascus to examine some old manuscripts, which he believed might contain references to one of his ancestors.

"Although I was born in Brashov," he said, "family records indicate that we had our beginnings elsewhere. You may think it snobbish, this delving into my background, but it is a hobby, which has absorbed me for many years. I am not looking for glory; only for facts."

"Nothing wrong with that," Craig said. "I envy you your colorful past."

"Is yours so dull, then?"

"Not dull…the colors just aren't so nice. I grew up in the Atlanta slums. Things were a little…rough when I was a kid."

"You weren't big enough to be tough."

Craig nodded, wondering why he didn't resent this second reference to his small size. He decided that it was because he liked the big man. Hofmanstahal wasn't insolent, just candid and direct.

"I read a lot," Craig went on. "My interest in astronomy led me into navigation while I was in the Navy. After I was mustered out I stayed at sea rather than go back to what I'd left."

They continued to converse in low, earnest voices for the remainder of the afternoon. Always above them the white gulls circled.

"Beautiful, aren't they?" asked Craig.

Hofmanstahal looked up. His pale eyes narrowed. "Scavengers! See the wicked eyes, the cruel beaks! Pah!"

Craig shrugged. "Let's eat. And hadn't you better do something for that cut under your eye?"

Hofmanstahal shook his massive head. "You eat, if you wish. I am not hungry." He touched his tongue to the dribble of blood that ran down his cheek.

THEY kept track of the days by cutting notches in the gunwale. There were two notches when Craig first began to wonder about Hofmanstahal.

They had arranged a system of rationing for food and water. It was far from being a strict ration, for there was plenty for both of them.

But Craig never saw Hofmanstahal eat.

The Rumanian, Craig thought, was a big man, he should certainly have an equally big appetite.

"I prefer," said Hofmanstahal, when Craig asked about it, "to take my meals at night."

Craig let it pass, assuming that the big man had a digestive disorder, or perhaps was one of those unfortunates who possess inhibitions about eating in front of others. Not that the latter seemed likely, considering Hofmanstahal's amiably aggressive personality and the present unusual circumstances but, on the other hand, what did it matter? Let him eat standing on his head if he wanted to.

Next morning, when Craig opened the food locker to get his share, the food supply was apparently undiminished.

The morning after that, the same thing.

Another notch. Five days, now. And Craig found something else to puzzle about. He was eating well; yet he felt himself sinking deeper and deeper into a strange, uncaring lethargy, as if he were well on his way toward starvation.

He took advantage of the abundance of food to eat more than was his wont. It didn't help.

Hofmanstahal, on the other hand, greeted each day with a sparkling eye and a spate of good-humored talk.

Both men by now had beards.

Craig detested his, for it itched. Hofmanstahal was favoring his, combing it with his fingers, already training the mustache with insistent twiddlings of thumb and forefinger.

Craig lay wearily in the bow and watched.

"Hofmanstahal," he said. "You're not starving yourself on my account, are you? It isn't necessary, you know."

"No, my friend. I have never eaten better."

"But you've hardly touched the stores."

"Ah!" Hofmanstahal flexed his big muscles. Sunlight flickered along the golden hair that fuzzed his torso. "It is the inactivity. My appetite suffers."

ANOTHER notch. Craig continued to wonder. Each day, each hour, found him weaker, more listless. He lay in the bow of the boat, soaking in the warmth of the sun, his eyes opaque, his body limp. Sometimes he let one hand dangle in the cool water; but the appearance of ugly, triangular shark fins put a stop to that.

"They are like all of nature, the sharks," Hofmanstahal said. "They rend and kill, and give nothing in return for the food they so brutally take. They can offer only their very bodies, which are in turn devoured by larger creatures. And on and on. The world is not a pretty place, my friend."

"Are men so different?"

"Men are the worst of all."

Seven notches, now. Craig was growing weaker. He was positive by now that Hofmanstahal was simply not eating.

There were nine notches on the gunwale when Craig found that Hofmanstahal *was* eating, after all.

It was night, and the sea was rougher than it had been. The *slap-slap* of waves against the hull wakened Craig from a deep, trancelike sleep. That, and the oppressive feeling of a nearby presence.

He stirred, felt the presence withdraw. Through half-shut eyes he saw Hofmanstahal, darkly silhouetted against a sky ablaze with stars.

"You were crying out in your sleep, my friend." The big man's voice was solicitous. "Nightmare?"

"My throat...stinging, burning. I..."

"The salt air. You will be all right in the morning."

Craig's face felt like a numb mask of clay. It was an effort to move his lips. "I think—I think I'm going—to die."

"No. You are not going to die. You must not. If you die, I die."

Craig thought about that. The rocking of the boat was gentle, soothing. A warmth stole over him, though the night was cool. He was weak, but comfortable; fearful, yet content. Head back, breathing easily, he let himself become aware of the glory of the heavens.

The constellation Perseus was slanting toward the western horizon, and Craig noted almost unconsciously, with the skill of long practice, that the variable star Algol was at its maximum brilliancy. Algol—the ghoul.

The thought lingered. It turned over and over in his mind, as his unconscious seemed to examine it for some hidden meaning.

Then, abruptly, the thought surged up into his conscious mind.

And he knew.

He lifted himself up to his elbows, supporting himself weakly.

"Hofmanstahal," he said, "you're a vampire. Aren't you?"

The other's chuckle was deep and melodious in the darkness.

"Answer me, Hofmanstahal. Are you a vampire?"

"Yes."

CRAIG had fainted. Now it was as if layer after layer of blackness were being removed, bringing him closer to the light with every moment. A tiny sullen orange disk glowed in the darkness, expanding, increasing in brightness until it filled the world.

The blackness was gone, and he was staring up into the blinding, brassy heart of the sun.

He gasped and turned his head away.

There was music. Someone whistling a German folk tune.

Hofmanstahal...

Hofmanstahal sat in the stern, his brawny gold-fuzzed forearms resting on his knees.

The whistling stopped.

"Good morning, my friend. You have had a good, long rest."

Craig stared, his lips working. Far above a gull called harshly, and was answered by one skimming at water level.

Hofmanstahal smiled. "You mustn't look at me that way. I'm almost harmless, I assure you." He laughed gently. "Things could be much worse, you know. Suppose, for example, I had been a werewolf. Eh?"

He waited a moment.

"Oh, yes, Lycanthropy is real—as real as those gulls out there. Or—more fitting, perhaps—as real as those sharks. Once, in Paris, I lived for three months with a young woman who was a public bath attendant by day and a werewolf by night. She would choose her victims by their—"

CRAIG listened numbly, aware that Hofmanstahal was merely making idle talk. The story of the female werewolf turned into an anecdote, patently untrue. Hofmanstahal chuckled at it, and seemed disappointed when Craig did not. There was a certain sensitive shyness about the big Rumanian,

Craig thought…a sensitive vampire! Aware of Craig's revulsion, he was camouflaging the situation with a flood of words.

"—And when the gendarme saw that the bullet, which had killed her was an ordinary lead one, he said, 'Messieurs, you have done this *pauvre jeune fille* a grave injustice.' Ha! The moment was a sad one for me, but—"

"Stop it!" Craig gasped. "Go turn yourself into a bat or something and flyaway. Just get out of my sight…my blood in your stomach…"

He tried to turn away, and his elbows slipped. His shoulder blades thumped the bottom of the boat. He lay there, eyes closed, and his throat thickened as if he wanted to laugh and vomit at the same time.

"I cannot turn myself into a bat, my friend. Ugly little creatures—" Hofmanstahal sighed heavily. "Nor do I sleep in a coffin. Nor does daylight kill me, as you can see. All that is superstition. Superstition! Do you know that my grandfather died with a white ash stake through his heart?" His beard tilted angrily. "Believe me, we variants have more to fear from the ignorant and superstitious than they from us. There are so many of them, and so few of us."

Craig said, "You won't touch me again!"

"Ah, but I must."

"I'm still strong enough to fight you off."

"But not strong enough to get at the food if I choose to prevent you."

Craig shook his head. "I'll throw myself overboard!"

"That I cannot permit. Now, why not submit to the inevitable? Each day, I will supply you with your ration of food; each night, you will supply me with mine. A symbiotic relationship. What could be fairer?"

"Beast! Monster! *I will not*—"

Hofmanstahal sighed, and looked out over the tossing sea. "Monster. Always they say that of us; they, who feed off the burned flesh of living creatures."

IT WAS the face of his father, stern and reproving, that Craig always saw before him during those long nights in the lifeboat. His father, who had been a Baptist minister. When the lifeboat drifted on a sea that was like glass, reflecting the stars with such clarity that the boat might have been suspended in a vast star-filled sphere, and Craig felt the warm, moist lips of the vampire at his throat—then conscience arose in the form of his father.

Well...he wasn't submitting willingly. Not at first. But the food had been withheld until his belly twisted with hunger and he cried out with parched lips for water. Then, shudderingly, he had allowed the vampire to feed.

It was not as bad as he had expected. An acute, stinging sensation as the sharp canines pricked the flesh (strange, that he had not noticed before how *sharp* they were); then numbness as the anesthetic venom did its work. The venom must have been a hypnotic. As the numbness spread toward his face, and his lips and cheeks became chill, strange colors danced before his eyes, blending and twining in cloudy patterns that sent his thoughts wandering down incomprehensible byways. He was part of Hofmanstahal. Hofmanstahal was part of him. The feeling was almost lascivious.

And each time it was less painful, less shocking, till finally it was mere routine.

Strangely, his conscience did not torment him during the day. The comfortable warmth and lassitude that before had only touched him now enveloped him completely. His thoughts were vague; memory tended to slip away from what had gone before, and to evade what was to come. The sea, the sky, the wheeling gulls were beautiful. And Hofmanstahal, vampire or not, was an interesting conversationalist.

"You are pale, friend Craig," he would say. "Perhaps I have been too greedy. Do you know, with that wan face and the beard, you remind me of a poet I knew in Austria. For a long time he was one of my favorite companions. But perhaps you did not know that we prefer certain donors to others. Believe me, we are not the indiscriminate gluttons that literature would have you think."

"How—did you become as you are?"

"How did I, Eric Hofmanstahal, become a vampire? That is a question with broad implications. I can tell you that my people were vampires, but that leaves unanswered the question of our origin. This I cannot tell you, though I have searched deeply into the matter. There are legends, of course, but they are contradictory." Hofmanstahal stroked his beard and seemed lost in thought.

"Some say," he went on, after a moment, "that when Homo sapiens and the ape branched from a common ancestor, there was a third strain, which was so despised by both that it was driven into obscurity. Others maintain that we came to Earth from another planet, in prehistoric times. There is even mention of a species, which was quite different from man but which, because of man's dominance over the earth, imitated him until it developed a physical likeness to him. Then there is the fanciful notion that we are servants of the Devil—one battalion among his legions, created by him to spread sorrow and misery throughout the ages of the world.

"Legends! We have been persecuted, imprisoned, burned alive; we have been classified as maniacs and perverts—all because our body chemistry is unlike that of man. We drink from the fountain of life while man feasts at the fleshpots of the dead; yet we are called monsters." He crumpled a biscuit in his powerful hand and cast the pieces upon the water, which immediately boiled with sharks.

"Man!" he said softly.

LIFE went on. Craig ate. Hofmanstahal fed. And horror diminished with familiarity.

There were only the two of them, under the vast sky, rising and falling gently to the whim of the sea. The horizon was the edge of their world. No other existed. Night and day merged into gray sameness. Sea and sky were vague, warm reflections;

the motion of the boat soothed. This was peace. There was no thought of resistance left in Craig. Hofmanstahal's "symbiosis" became a way of life; then life itself.

There was time in plenty to gaze up at the stars, a pleasure, which everyday exigencies had so often denied him. And there was strange, dark companionship; lips' that sought his throat and drained away all thoughts of urgency or violent action, leaving him exhausted and somehow thrilled. It was peace. It was satisfaction. It was fulfillment.

Fear was lost in stupor; revulsion, in a certain sensuality. Hofmanstahal's nightly visit was no longer a thing of horror, but the soft arrival of a friend whom he wanted to help with all his being, and who was in turn helping him. Night and day they exchanged life; and the life they nurtured became a single flow and purpose between them. Craig was the quiescent vessel of life, which Hofmanstahal filled every day, so that life might build itself against the coming of night and the return of its essence to Hofmanstahal.

Day and night marched above them toward the pale horizon that circumscribed their world. In their world values had changed, and the fact of change been forgotten.

Still, deep in his mind, Craig's conscience wailed. Legend, history, the church, all at one time or another had said that vampires were evil. He was submitting to a vampire; therefore, he was submitting to evil. Food or no food, the Reverend Craig would never have submitted. He would have sharpened a stake or cast a silver bullet—

But there were no such things here. His father's face rose before him to tell him that this did not matter. He sought to drive it away, but it remained. During the moments of nightly meeting, of warmth and strange intimacy, it glared down upon them brighter than the moon. But Hofmanstahal's back was always turned to it; and Craig, in all his weakness and agony and ecstasy and indecision, did not mention it.

THEY had forgotten to carve the notches on the gunwale. Neither was certain now how long they had been adrift.

There came a day, however, when Hofmanstahal was forced to cut down Craig's ration of food.

"I am sorry," he said, "but you can see for yourself that it is necessary."

"We're so near the end of our supplies, then?"

"I am sorry," Hofmanstahal repeated. "Yes, we are nearing the end of your supplies...and if yours end, so will mine eventually."

"I don't really mind," Craig whispered. "I'm seldom really hungry now. At first, even the full rations left me unsatisfied, but now I don't even like the taste of the food. I suppose it's because I'm getting no exercise."

Hofmanstahal's smile was gentle. "Perhaps. Perhaps not. We must keep a sharp lookout for ships. If one does not come soon, we will starve, though, of course, I will now cut down my own rations as well as yours."

"I don't care."

"My poor Craig, when you regain your strength you will care very much. Like me, you will want to live and go on living."

"Maybe. But now I feel that dying would be easy and pleasant. Better, maybe, than going back to the world."

"The world is evil, yes; but the will to live in it drives all of us."

Craig lay motionless and wondered, with a clarity of mind he had not experienced in many, many days, whether he dreaded going back to the world because the world was evil, or whether it was because he felt that he himself was tainted, unfit to mix with human beings again.

...And Hofmanstahal might be a problem. Should he be reported to the authorities? No, for then they would know about Craig.

But was all that had happened so disgraceful, so reprehensible? Had Craig had any other choice but to do what he had done?

None.

His conscience, in the form of his father, screamed agony.

Well, then perhaps Hofmanstahal would try to force him to continue the relationship. Had he—*pleased* the Rumanian? He felt that he had...

But surely gentle, considerate Hofmanstahal, the sensitive vampire, would not try to force—

Craig's mind rebelled against such practical thoughts. They required too much effort. It was easier not to think at all—to lie as he had lain for so many days, peaceful, relaxed, uncaring.

Clarity of mind faded into the gray sameness of day and night. He ate. Hofmanstahal fed.

HE was scarcely conscious when Hofmanstahal spotted the smoke on the horizon. The big man lifted him up so that he could see it. It was a ship, and it was coming in their direction.

"So—now it is over." Hofmanstahal's voice was soft; his hands were warm on Craig's shoulders. "So it ends—our little idyll." The hands tightened. "My friend...my friend, before the ship comes, the men and the noise, the work and the worry and all that goes with it, let us for the last time—"

His head bent, his lips found Craig's throat with their almost sexual avidity.

Craig shivered. Over the Rumanian's shoulder he could see the ship approaching, a dot on the horizon. There would be men aboard.

Men! Normalcy and sanity, cities and machines and half-forgotten values, coming nearer and nearer over the tossing sea, beneath the brassy sky, from the real world of men that lay somewhere beyond the horizon...

Men! Like himself, like his father, who hovered shouting his disgust.

And he, lying in the arms of—God, God, *what if they should see him!*

He kicked. He threw his arms about. He found strength he hadn't known he had, and threshed and flailed and shrieked with it.

The lifeboat rocked. A foot caught Hofmanstahal in the midriff. The vampire's arms flew wide and he staggered back with a cry:

"Craig—"

The backs of his knees struck the gunwale—the one with meaningless notches carved in it. His arms lashed as he strove to regain his balance. His eyes locked with Craig's, shock in them. Then he plunged backward into the sea.

The sharks rejected him as food, but not before they had killed him.

Craig found himself weeping in the bottom of the boat, his face in slime. And saying hoarsely again and again, "Eric, I'm sorry—"

IT seemed a very long time before the ship came close enough for him to make out the moving figures on the deck. It seemed so long because of the thoughts and half-formed images that were racing through his brain.

A new awareness was coming over him in a hot flood, an awareness of—

Of the one thing popularly believed about vampires that must have solid foundation in fact.

Had the venom done it? He didn't know. He didn't care.

He lay weakly, watching the steamer through half-closed eyes. Sailors lined the rails, their field glasses trained on him.

He wondered if they could see his father. No, of course not—that had all been hallucination. Besides, a moment ago his father had fled.

It was a Navy ship, a destroyer. He was glad of that. He knew the Navy. The men would be healthy. Strenuous duty would make them sleep soundly.

And at the end of its voyage lay the whole pulsing world.

Craig licked his lips.

THE END

THE STATEMENT OF RANDOLPH CARTER

By H. P. Lovecraft

From 1920, here is one of our favorite short Lovecraft classics…

AGAIN I SAY, I do not know what has become of Harley Warren, though I think—almost hope—that he is in peaceful oblivion, if there be anywhere so blessed a thing. It is true that I have for five years been his closest friend, and a partial sharer of his terrible researches into the unknown. I will not deny, though my memory is uncertain and indistinct, that this witness of yours may have seen us together as he says, on the Gainsville pike, walking toward Big Cypress Swamp, at half past 11 on that awful night. That we bore electric lanterns, spades, and a curious coil of wire with attached instruments, I will even affirm; for these things all played a part in the single hideous scene which remains burned into my shaken recollection. But of what followed, and of the reason I was found alone and dazed on the edge of the swamp next morning, I must insist that I know nothing save what I have told you over and over again. You say to me that there is nothing in the swamp or near it which could form the setting of that frightful episode. I reply that I knew nothing beyond what I saw. Vision or nightmare it may have been—vision or nightmare I fervently hope it was— yet it is all that my mind retains of what took place in those shocking hours after we left the sight of men. And why Harley Warren did not return, he or his shade—or some nameless thing I cannot describe—alone can tell.

As I have said before, the weird studies of Harley Warren were well known to me, and to some extent shared by me. Of his vast collection of strange, rare books on forbidden subjects I have read all that are written in the languages of which I am master; but these are few as compared with those in languages I cannot understand. Most, I believe, are in Arabic; and the fiend-inspired book which brought on the end—the book which he carried in his pocket out of the world—was written in characters whose like I never saw elsewhere. Warren would never tell me just what was in that book. As to the nature of our studies— must I say again that I no longer retain full comprehension? It seems to me rather merciful that I do not, for they were terrible studies, which I pursued more through reluctant fascination than through actual inclination. Warren always dominated me, and sometimes I feared him. I remember how I shuddered at his facial expression on the night before the awful happening, when he talked so incessantly of his theory, why certain corpses never decay, but rest firm and fat in their tombs for a thousand years. But I do not fear him now, for I suspect that he has known horrors beyond my ken. Now I fear for him.

Once more I say that I have no clear idea of our object on that night. Certainly, it had much to do with something in the book which Warren carried with him—that ancient book in undecipherable characters which had come to him from India a month before—but I swear I do not know what it was that we expected to find. Your witness says he saw us at half past 11 on the Gainsville pike, headed for Big Cypress Swamp. This is probably true, but I have no distinct memory of it. The picture seared into my soul is of one scene only, and the hour must have been long after midnight; for a waning crescent moon was high in the vaporous heavens.

The place was an ancient cemetery; so ancient that I trembled at the manifold signs of immemorial years. It was in a deep, damp hollow, overgrown with rank grass, moss, and curious creeping weeds, and filled with a vague stench which my idle fancy associated absurdly with rotting stone. On every hand were the signs of neglect and decrepitude, and I seemed haunted by the notion that Warren and I were the first living creatures to invade a lethal silence of centuries. Over the valley's rim a wan, waning crescent moon peered through the noisome vapors that seemed to emanate from unheard of catacombs, and by its feeble, wavering beams I could distinguish a repellent array of antique slabs, urns, cenotaphs, and mausoleum facades; all crumbling, moss-grown, and moisture-stained, and partly concealed by the gross luxuriance of the unhealthy vegetation.

My first vivid impression of my own presence in this terrible necropolis concerns the act of pausing with Warren before a certain half-obliterated sepulcher, and of throwing down some burdens which we seemed to have been carrying. I now observed that I had with me an electric lantern and two spades, whilst my companion was supplied with a similar lantern and a portable telephone outfit. No word was uttered, for the spot and the task seemed known to us; and without delay we seized our spades and commenced to clear away the grass, weeds, and drifted earth from the flat, archaic mortuary. After uncovering the entire surface, which consisted of three immense granite slabs, we stepped back some distance to survey the charnel scene; and Warren appeared to make some mental calculations. Then he returned to the sepulcher, and using his spade as a lever, sought to pry up the slab lying nearest to a stony ruin which may have been a monument in its day. He did not succeed, and motioned to me to come to his assistance. Finally our combined strength loosened the stone, which we raised and tipped to one side.

The removal of the slab revealed a black aperture, from which rushed an effluence of miasmal gases so nauseous that we started back in horror. After an interval, however, we approached the pit again, and found the exhalations less unbearable. Our lanterns disclosed the top of a flight of stone steps, dripping with some detestable ichor of the inner earth, and bordered by moist walls encrusted with niter. And now for the first time my memory records verbal discourse, Warren addressing me at length in his mellow tenor voice; a voice singularly unperturbed by our awesome surroundings.

"I'm sorry to have to ask you to stay on the surface," he said, "but it would be a crime to let anyone with your frail nerves go down there. You can't imagine, even from what you have read and from what I've told you, the things I shall have to see and do. It's fiendish work, Carter, and I doubt if any man without ironclad sensibilities could ever see it through and come up alive and sane. I don't wish to offend you, and Heaven knows I'd be glad enough to have you with me; but the responsibility is in a certain sense mine, and I couldn't drag a bundle of nerves like you down to probable death or madness. I tell you, you can't imagine what the thing is really like! But I promise to keep you informed over the telephone of every move—you see I've enough wire here to reach to the center of the earth and back!"

I can still hear, in memory, those coolly spoken words; and I can still remember my remonstrances. I seemed desperately anxious to accompany my friend into those sepulchral depths, yet he proved inflexibly obdurate. At one time he threatened to abandon the expedition if I remained insistent; a threat which proved effective, since he alone held the key to the thing. All this I can still remember, though I no longer know what manner of thing we sought. After he had obtained my reluctant acquiescence in his design, Warren picked up the reel of wire and adjusted the instruments. At his nod I took one of the latter and seated myself upon an aged, discolored gravestone close by the newly uncovered aperture. Then he shook my hand, shouldered the coil of wire, and disappeared within that indescribable ossuary.

For a minute I kept sight of the glow of his lantern, and heard the rustle of the wire as he laid it down after him; but the glow soon disappeared abruptly, as if a turn in the stone staircase had been encountered, and the sound died away almost as quickly. I was alone, yet bound to the unknown depths by those magic strands whose insulated surface lay green beneath the struggling beams of that waning crescent moon.

I constantly consulted my watch by the light of my electric lantern, and listened with feverish anxiety at the receiver of the telephone; but for more than a quarter of an hour heard nothing. Then a faint clicking came from the instrument, and I called down to my friend in a tense voice. Apprehensive as I was, I was nevertheless unprepared for the words which came up from that uncanny vault in accents more alarmed and quivering than any I had heard before from Harley Warren. He who had so calmly left me a little while previously, now called from below in a shaky whisper more portentous than the loudest shriek:

"God! If you could see what I am seeing!"

I could not answer. Speechless, I could only wait. Then came the frenzied tones again:

"Carter, it's terrible—monstrous—unbelievable!"

This time my voice did not fail me, and I poured into the transmitter a flood of excited questions. Terrified, I continued to repeat, "Warren, what is it? What is it?"

Once more came the voice of my friend, still hoarse with fear, and now apparently tinged with despair:

"I can't tell you, Carter! It's too utterly beyond thought—I dare not tell you—no man could know it and live—Great God! I never dreamed of this!"

Stillness again, save for my now incoherent torrent of shuddering inquiry. Then the voice of Warren in a pitch of wilder consternation:

"Carter! for the love of God, put back the slab and get out of this if you can! Quick!—leave everything else and make for the outside—it's your only chance! Do as I say, and don't ask me to explain!"

I heard, yet was able only to repeat my frantic questions. Around me were the tombs and the darkness and the shadows; below me, some peril beyond the radius of the human imagination. But my friend was in greater danger than I, and through my fear I felt a vague resentment that he should deem me capable of deserting him under such circumstances. More clicking, and after a pause a piteous cry from Warren:

"Beat it! For God's sake, put back the slab and beat it, Carter!"

Something in the boyish slang of my evidently stricken companion unleashed my faculties. I formed and shouted a resolution, "Warren, brace up! I'm coming down!" But at this offer the tone of my auditor changed to a scream of utter despair:

"Don't! You can't understand! It's too late—and my own fault. Put back the slab and run—there's nothing else you or anyone can do now!"

The tone changed again, this time acquiring a softer quality, as of hopeless resignation. Yet it remained tense through anxiety for me.

"Quick—before it's too late!"

I tried not to heed him; tried to break through the paralysis which held me, and to fulfil my vow to rush down to his aid. But his next whisper found me still held inert in the chains of stark horror.

"Carter—hurry! It's no use—you must go—better one than two—the slab—"

A pause, more clicking, then the faint voice of Warren:

"Nearly over now—don't make it harder—cover up those damned steps and run for your life—you're losing time—so long, Carter—won't see you again."

Here Warren's whisper swelled into a cry; a cry that gradually rose to a shriek fraught with all the horror of the ages—

"Curse these hellish things—legions—my God! Beat it! Beat it! BEAT IT!"

After that was silence. I know not how many interminable eons I sat stupefied; whispering, muttering, calling, screaming into that telephone. Over and over again through those eons I whispered and muttered, called, shouted, and screamed, "Warren! Warren! Answer me—are you there?"

And then there came to me the crowning horror of all—the unbelievable, unthinkable, almost unmentionable thing. I have said that eons seemed to elapse after Warren shrieked forth his last despairing warning, and that only my own cries now broke the hideous silence. But after a while there was a further clicking in the receiver, and I strained my ears to listen. Again I called down, "Warren, are you there?" and in answer heard the thing which has brought this cloud over my mind. I do not try, gentlemen, to account for that thing—that voice—nor can I venture to describe it in detail, since the first words took away my consciousness and created a mental blank which reaches to the time of my awakening in the hospital. Shall I say that the voice was deep; hollow; gelatinous; remote; unearthly; inhuman; disembodied? What shall I say? It was the end of my experience, and is the end of my story. I heard it, and knew no more—heard it as I sat petrified in that unknown cemetery in the hollow, amidst the crumbling stones and the falling tombs, the rank vegetation and the miasmal vapors—heard it well up from the innermost depths of that damnable open sepulcher as I watched amorphous, necrophagous shadows dance beneath an accursed waning moon.

And this is what it said:

"You fool, Warren is DEAD!"

THE END

PURDY'S CIRCUS

By Franklin Gregory

It's a lot of fun to go to a circus. It isn't always so amusing when the circus comes to you.

WE tell you without malarkey that Morton Purdy, on that April afternoon in the big camera store across from Grand Central, met up with the Devil. It could have been no on else. Only the Devil would pull such a nasty trick.

Mr. Purdy, after foregoing Heaven only knows how many beers, had saved enough to buy a really superior lens for his enlarger. With the pleasant anticipation of a child in Disneyland, he peered at the gleaming optical display in the brightly-lighted show case.

"Coated?" the salesman inquired politely. "It's remarkable how a coated lens increases the brilliance of the image."

"What I'd like to afford," Mr. Purdy confided shyly, "is an apochromatic."

"I know just how you feel," the salesman agreed. "Superb definition."

Mr. Purdy regarded the salesman. It was nice for once to find, instead of the usual rude and hard-sell whippersnapper, someone who took a courteous interest. The man's eyes were dark, and also impish as if they knew a capital off-color joke. But they were urbane and wise and they smiled at Mr. Purdy as if they knew a good deal about him. Mr. Purdy had the unreasonable idea they knew about Agnes, too. It made him feel slightly uncomfortable.

Agnes was Mr. Purdy's cross, and it was she who had prompted his interest in photography.

"Morton," she had told him, "don't you think that if you had a hobby you wouldn't drink so much?"

Mr. Purdy hadn't felt he drank too much. It was simply that all of his life he had been lonely and had come to find a certain solace in the neighborhood taprooms. And all of his twenty years of marriage, Agnes Purdy had found fault with it. She was a persistent, forceful nag, and it was not the first time she had suggested a hobby. There was that birthday, for example, when she had given him a set of golf clubs and a club membership— only to learn too late about the 19th Hole.

But when Agnes gave him the enlarger for Christmas, she had scored. Mr. Purdy found immense satisfaction in making big pictures out of little ones. For one thing, the evenings he spent with the developing fluids under the yellow safe-light in the blacked-out kitchen were just so many evenings he could escape Mrs. Purdy's company. For another, when now he disappeared for a Saturday or Sunday, he could always explain he'd been out with his camera.

Whether the salesman knew about Agnes, he had reached a decision about Mr. Purdy.

"Tell you what," he said, glancing around to see if anyone was looking. "The store wouldn't like this, but you've got two hundred dollars and—"

Mr. Purdy was jolted. It was the exact amount in his wallet. The salesman smiled blandly.

"X-ray vision."

"Of course," agreed Mr. Purdy, blinking mildly behind his spectacles. "Superman."

"Better than that," the salesman grinned. "But even Superman can't live without the evil needful, y'know, and since I'm frightfully underpaid by these Scrooges... What I'm saying is, all these lenses are very nice, but—look here."

From his pocket he produced a small chamois sack and removed a shining metal cylinder about an inch long.

Mr. Purdy held it gingerly to the light—and caught his breath. Deep-set within the cylinder shone the loveliest lens imaginable.

"What—make is it?"

"Called a Spectre."

"German?"

"Ha. Even Zeiss, even Leitz can't make a lens like this. No, they're off the market a good many years. Fellow in Bohemia...lens-grinder...little family business, y'know...invented a secret abrasive. Secret died with him."

Mr. Purdy disliked under-the-counter schemes. He shifted his stance restlessly.

"Oh it's out of this world," the salesman pressed. "I tell you, it'll make your enlargements big as life and twice as real."

His eyes seemed even more impish.

Standing in the spring rain waiting for the Lexington Avenue bus, Mr. Purdy had a moment of doubt. He had no receipt, he'd paid no sales tax. What if he'd been swindled? But when he boarded the bus and re-examined the lens, he was reassured. And by the time he reached 67th and was walking east toward his apartment, he was feeling so pleased that he thought one little highball would do no harm to celebrate. It was so very seldom Mr. Purdy was really happy.

He was glowing pleasantly over his third in Joe's Bar & Grill when the inspiration struck him. He wondered he hadn't thought of it before. Why not, he considered, combine the pleasure of wetting his whistle with the other pleasure of making big ones out of little ones? He did not consider that this would defeat Mrs. Purdy's purpose. He only remembered that she never disturbed him when he was in his kitchen-dark room.

Arriving home with the bottle of rye concealed in his topcoat and feeling like a naughty schoolboy, Mr. Purdy was in luck. Mrs. Purdy's brief note advised him that she would be late and there was cold lamb in the frig.

If his hands trembled in hanging the blackout curtain over the window and in pouring the solutions into the trays, Mr. Purdy was not aware of it. Setting the enlarger on the kitchen table, he unscrewed the stock lens from the lens board and, with utmost care, inserted the new prize.

"Spectre," he mused. "What an unusual name."

A week earlier, on its last appearance at Madison Square Garden, Mr. Purdy had visited the circus and shot, and later developed, a couple of rolls of film. All his life the circus had thrilled him, and he was eager now to see how the pictures blew up. Sorting the negatives, he found the shot of "the incomparable, the irresistible, the one and only Lola Lark, aerialist supreme."

"And a dainty dish, too," Mr. Purdy smiled as he held the negative up. He had caught her with the telephoto lens just as she sat swinging, slim ankles crossed, on the high trapeze; a sprite in pink tights, brief ballet skirt and daring bodice.

It was a pity Agnes didn't have such a figure.

Wistfully recalling the lost opportunities of his lost youth, Mr. Purdy mixed another drink. Then he inserted the negative dull-side down in the negative carrier, slid the carrier into the enlarger, closed the lamp house, switched on the dim yellow safe-light and switched off the room light. Setting the lens at its largest opening, he turned on the enlarger lamp and began the precision focusing by lowering and raising the bellows.

For Mr. Purdy, like many another aficionado, this was always a breathless moment. Slowly the fuzzy blur of light and shadow on the white baseboard resolved into a large, clean image.

Mr. Purdy whistled softly. Lola's physical construction was even more sensational than the small negative had suggested.

"Big as life and twice as real, the man said," Mr. Purdy recalled as he examined the life-like definition produced by his new jewel. And he was just about to reach for his highball when the image appeared to stir. Ah-ah, he warned himself; must have jarred the table. But the image moved again; and now it seemed to grow. And this time Mr. Purdy did reach for his drink, gulped and shook his head with vigor.

"Haven't had that much."

And still the image grew...and grew, and moved, and grew some more; until, sitting pertly on the edge of the table, her lovely ankles still crossed and all of her near-nakedness illumined by only the faint glow of the safe-light, was the diminutive aerialist herself.

"Hi!" she said brightly.

"Uh," said Mr. Purdy as if he'd been socked in the stomach.

She glanced slowly around.

"Cozy," she said. "But d'ya always keep the kitchen this dark?"

Mr. Purdy tried to clear his head again by shaking it.

"No," he said, "I mean—"

He turned on the room light, thinking she might dissolve. But she was still there—more so, in fact. For now he saw what, from the distance between them at the circus he had been unable to define before: the saucy nose, the naughty eyes and the sheen of flaxen hair. Reaching out, he touched her to see if she were real.

"Hey mister, don't go gettin' fresh."

Mr. Purdy quickly drew back, but his eyes remained feasting on the suggestive hollow of her bodiced breasts.

"And quit starin' like a yokel," she commanded.

Her choice of words and gutter accent shocked Mr. Purdy.

"I'm sorry," he stammered. "It's only that I've never seen such—"

"Skip it," said Lola, pleased. Sliding off her perch, she prowled the kitchen.

"What's all this junk?"

"Photographic enlarging equipment," Mr. Purdy said.

She squinted at him.

"So you're one of these hypo hounds, huh? Ever try drinkin' the stuff? Hey! Don't tell me you got some real jig water there!" She smacked her lips. "Now we're getting somewhere. Be a sport, pal, and pour little Lola a quencher. Gawd, I feel like I been through a wringer."

"As a matter of fact," Mr. Purdy started to say. He mixed her a drink, and one for himself, then sagged into a kitchen chair. Lola Lark, the irresistible, drank long and noisily.

"Ahh, that's more like it!" she exclaimed when she'd emptied the glass. "But if I'm gonna stay in this pad, you'll have to lay in some Scotch."

She wiggled enticingly toward him, and it was all Mr. Purdy could bear.

"Y'know," she smiled, "you ain't such a bad sort. Have ya had that cute bald spot long?"

Mr. Purdy fidgeted. She sauntered to the window and pulled the blackout curtain aside.

"Say, kid, this looks like New York!"

"It is," said Mr. Purdy. "Sixty-seventh near Third."

She stared at him.

"Holy cow! I thought I was in Boston."

"You're supposed to be," Mr. Purdy said. "That's where the circus is."

"What happened? Did I miss the train?"

"I wouldn't know."

"Then how the devil did I get here with you?"

"Through that," Mr. Purdy sighed, nodding toward the enlarger. "And I do wish you would get back in it. My wife's coming home any moment and I don't know what she'll say if she finds you here and, uh, dressed like this."

Lola giggled. She was feeling the drink. She closed one eye and examined the enlarger.

"Y'mean I came through that li'l ol' thing? Ah honey, you are a card!"

With that, she sat down on Mr. Purdy's lap, wrapped a white arm around his neck and planted a spectacular kiss on his bald spot.

If Mr. Purdy's conscience stirred uneasily, he himself did not. Her bottom was warm and exciting; not even from the time of courting Mrs. Purdy could he recall such a pleasant sensation. Nor did he move when Lola asked:

"How's it work?"

"The enlarger? Oh, you press the lever." Lola reached out and pressed the lever. "And you take out that little pan." The negative was still in the carrier and she held it up to the light.

"Oh!" she cried with delight. "It's a picture of li'l ol' me! It's awf'ly good."

Mr. Purdy beamed. Lola noticed the other negatives and picked one up at random.

"Why it's Susie the Snake Charmer!" She picked up another. "And here's the Bo-Bo clowns!" She picked up a third. "And my gawd, if it ain't Stevie and his tiger—" She looked at Mr. Purdy wide-eyed. "Honey, can you bring *them* through, too?"

"We-ll," Mr. Purdy began. And at that inconvenient moment, the kitchen door swung open and the formidable Mrs. Purdy—big as life and just as real with no aid from the optical science—stood in the doorway. For a long moment there was a most embarrassing silence. Then Mr. Purdy pushed Lola off his lap and got up.

"I didn't hear you come in, dear."

Mrs. Purdy sniffed grimly.

"I should rather think not. And what, please, is this hussy doing in my kitchen?"

"Well," Mr. Purdy gulped, "it's like this—"

"And dressed like that!" Mrs. Purdy blazed.

"You see—" Mr. Purdy tried again.

"And drinking!" Mrs. Purdy accused. And then Mr. Purdy witnessed a sight he'd never dreamed could happen. Agnes Purdy's fleshy lower lip trembled, her large eyes filled with tears, and she burst out sobbing.

"Oh Morton! To think I've lived with you all these years and trusted you so and stood by you in trouble—" Mr. Purdy could not recall ever being in serious trouble, unless it was Mrs. Purdy. "And all this time—" Mrs. Purdy wailed.

Her woeful look made Mr. Purdy wince. Then, her boxcar frame still shaking with sobs, she turned and staggered tragically across the living room, through the hall and into her bedroom where she closed the door.

Lola whistled.

"What an act!"

Mr. Purdy was dazed.

For some minutes they could hear Mrs. P. banging and slamming about. Once Mr. P. set down his glass, got up and went to the bedroom door. When he returned, he whispered in awe:

"I think...she's packing."

"Have a drink," said Lola.

"Maybe I ought to comfort her," Mr. Purdy said after a while. He started up, but Lola's cool hand detained him.

"Don't be a dope, Morty. You jus' think it's your duty. Ya ask me, you're one of these Caspar Milquetoasts an' you'd be better off rid of her."

"But what would I do?"

Lola flashed a blinding smile.

"Ya got me, ain'tcha?" And while Mr. Purdy was digesting that, Mrs. Purdy emerged from the hall, flounced through the living room and loomed up at the kitchen door. She carried two suitcases and she appeared her old indomitable self.

"You miserable worm! All those weekends you said you were taking pictures, ha! At your age a Lothario! You don't kid me, Mr. Morton Purdy. I'm going home to Mother."

As the outer door slammed behind her, Lola exploded with giggles.

"Can you tie that? An old battle wagon like her goin' home to Mama! That tops 'em all!"

And because it was really so utterly absurd, and perhaps too because of the sociable warmth inside and out, Mr. Purdy exploded with laughter, too.

It is pertinent, but not very chivalrous, to report on the naughty, affectionate night that Mr. Purdy spent in the arms of the one and only Lola. And when in the morning she whipped up the fluffiest batch of waffles ever to tempt his tongue, Mr. Purdy considered himself a fortunate man. Never had Mrs. P. been famous for her cookery.

"Of course," he suggested, eyeing Lola's scanty attire, "I'd better get you some clothes. You can hardly appear in the street like that."

Lola smiled lazily.

"Anything wrong with staying right here, lover boy?" she teased.

"I only meant—"

Lola wrote down her sizes.

"And, oh cert. Almost forgot. Size five pantie."

Mr. Purdy was still blushing when he went out. But when he reached the street and the reality of taxi horns and stinking garbage trucks and bawling children assailed him, he stood for several minutes in doubt. There had been the lens and the strange man who sold it to him. And of course as a kid he'd read "Through the Looking Glass" and somewhere he'd heard of magic mirrors and that Catherine de Medici had one in which she saw everything that happened in France. But it was all nonsense, really.

He had a slight headache and stopped in at Joe's Bar & Grill for a beer. Well then, if it was nonsense, what did it leave? Nightmare? Delirium tremens? Reaching for his change, he found the note. "Size 9 dress, size 34 bra." That was real enough.

He went to the phone, dropped a dime in the coin box and dialed his number, half-hoping, half-fearing to hear Agnes' voice. It was Lola who answered. With a pleasant sigh, he went about the business of shopping.

Fingering with the usual masculine embarrassment the nylon dainties, Mr. Purdy began to realize how horridly humdrum his marriage had been. A man deserved better than that out of life. He was whistling softly a half hour later when he stopped at the liquor store. There was every prospect for a most delicious repetition of last night and he was still whistling when, arms laden with packages, he stepped into the elevator.

"Got visitors, Mr. Purdy?" asked the operator.

"Uh—yes, matter of fact."

"Got a nice voice, that'n," the operator grinned. "Thanked me real pretty through the door, she did, when I brung up the mail."

"My wife's niece," Mr. Purdy said stiffly and without much originality.

"Yeah?" The lad was leering. "And when's *she* comin' back?"

Mr. Purdy was still thinking about reporting the insolent fellow to the super when he inserted his key in the lock. But as the door swung in, all thought of reporting anything to anybody vanished. In the center of the living room, its huge handsome head cradled in its great striped forepaws, sprawled the biggest tiger, Mr. P. would swear, ever to leave its native home in Bengal.

Mr. Purdy congealed. The tiger lifted its head and stared at him with large, curious eyes. Mr. Purdy held his breath. The tiger began a yawn, baring long red tongue and sharp, white incisors. Mr. Purdy continued to hold his breath. The yawn grew larger. Then Lola came out of the kitchen.

"Oh, back already? Good. I'll take the things. Get the Scotch? Fine. Want a drink?"

"I think," said Mr. Purdy, not taking his eyes from the tiger, "I do." He nodded toward the animal. "Tell me, it isn't real, is it?"

A man's bass voice called from the direction of the bathroom and Mr. Purdy jumped nervously.

"Ho, Lola! Is that him? Tell him we need twenty pounds of horsemeat."

Lola smiled her sweetest.

"We got guests," she said innocently.

Because there was no other support, Mr. Purdy sank into a chair, careful to select the one farthest from the tiger.

"So I gather," he said numbly. "Lola," he accused, "have you been monkeying with the enlarger?"

Before she could reply, the owner of the male voice appeared. He was tall, lithe, handsome, and because he was stripped to the waist Mr. Purdy could see his bulging biceps and powerful chest. He had a clipped, jaunty mustache; half his face was lathered with Mr. Purdy's shaving cream, and in one hand he wielded Mr. Purdy's razor.

"And listen, Mac," he said to Mr. Purdy. "U.S. inspected. Sonny's got a weak stomach."

Of the numerous turbulent emotions seething in Mr. Purdy's bosom—shock, fear, confusion—it was his sense of outrage that emerged dominant. He did not at all crave strange men and strange tigers barging into the privacy of his home; especially they did not appeal to him when he had planned a sybaritic weekend with a luscious and curvaceous blonde. With the greatest distaste, Mr. Purdy stared at the intruder.

"The name," he said frigidly, "is Morton...Mr. Morton Purdy."

"Okay, Mac. Mortie it is. I'm Steve."

"Captain Stephen Stevens," Lola put in, proudly accenting the title. "The famous wild animal trainer." She went back to the kitchen.

Mr. Purdy nodded toward the tiger.

"Is that...uh, is that beast tame?"

"Who, Sonny? Well now, it all depends what you call tame," the captain answered heartily, slashing off a hunk of beard. "When he's well fed, he's gentle as a lamb. So if you don't mind pushing off for that horsemeat..."

Mr. Purdy's annoyance increased. Not even by Agnes had he liked being shoved around.

"But my heavens, man," he said, asserting himself, "where does one get horsemeat?"

146

"Why," said the captain, "every supermarket carries it in one-pound packages. Thirty-two cents a pound. Frozen, y'know, old bean. So if you'd just pop off and get it. Takes time for it to unfreeze, y'know, and we wouldn't want Sonny to miss his mealtime, would we?"

"What would happen if he did?" Mr. Purdy asked.

"What would happen? Why, sir, first Sonny would begin to pace. And then he'd begin to growl, quiet like. And after that, he'd start roaring. You could hear him a mile."

This appalling prospect left Mr. Purdy in deep thought. Too well did he know the hard-heartedness of apartment house superintendents; too well he knew how scarce apartments were.

"And while you're at it, Mac, you better get forty pounds. Tomorrow's Sunday, y'know, and the stores are closed."

"You can't mean to keep that beast here that long?" Mr. P. cried in agonizing alarm.

"Where else would I keep him?" asked Captain Stevens logically. "You wouldn't want to park Sonny in a dirty old zoo, would you? And anyway, how'd you get him out of here without the super knowing?"

For a long moment, Mr. Purdy was silent.

"Why can't you get the meat?" he asked at last.

"In this rig?" Captain Stevens glanced down at his gaudy red pants, striped with a wide gold braid. "Besides," he added, closing the subject, "I don't have any money with me."

Mr. Purdy mentally calculated that forty pounds of horsemeat at 32 cents per pound came to $12.80. With an audible sigh, he got up and reached for his hat. Captain Stevens called to Lola in the kitchen:

"Ho, Lola! Has Ella come through yet?" And almost immediately from the kitchen a new voice sounded:

"My land! Is that you, Lola? I thought I never would make it."

Peeking into the kitchen, Mr. Purdy beheld the fattest woman imaginable. And because she was dressed in a short, frilly school-girlish dress, the rolls of pink flesh overlaying her cheeks and jowls and arms and bosom and calves seemed utterly obscene. She sat on a chair, panting laboriously. In the other chair sat Lola, adjusting another negative into the enlarger.

"No!" shouted the horrified Mr. Purdy. "No, Lola! You just can't do this to me! This is no boarding house!"

Lola pouted.

"You wouldn't want your li'l Lola lonesome, would you? And when I was so nice to you last night?"

Mr. Purdy hesitated. Hesitating, he was lost.

"I didn't figure on any more than just us two," he said forlornly.

Lola reached up and pinched his cheek.

"Don't you worry," she assured him. "We'll fix that tonight. Now be a nice Morty, and go get the horsemeat."

The horsemeat was heavy and so were Mr. Purdy's spirits.

"Whatcha feedin', a menagerie?" the supermarket checker grinned.

Mr. Purdy tried to smile.

He'd have to make another trip for the groceries, and Heaven only knew how much that fat woman would eat. And Heaven only knew, too, what to expect when he reached home again.

At first, as he re-entered the apartment, things seemed the same. And then he saw Lola kneeling on the living room floor—and he dropped the sacks. The packaged meat spilled out and at once Sonny trotted up and began sniffing. Captain Stevens followed.

"Good lad, you got it. But I say, don't give it to Sonny all at once. He'll get indigestion."

Mr. Purdy was not listening. Instead, his eyes were still riveted on Lola. She had removed the enlarger from the kitchen and plugged it into a living room socket, and now—surrounded by an assortment of negatives—she was inserting the pan in the carrier.

"No more, no more!" Mr. Purdy screamed, running toward her. "My God, woman, no more!"

He was too late. An explosion, a puff of smoke—and a tiny coupe stood in the center of the room, its motor still racing and its exhaust backfiring. The door opened and out stepped the world-famous clown, Bo-Bo. And after him stepped another clown; and then another—

And as each painted buffoon materialized, Lola called:

"Hi, Bob, Hi, Diz. Hi, Norbert, the drinks are right over there. Hi, Perce, glad ya could make it. Hi, Clarence—"

There were thirteen of them finally, not counting the midget who popped out at the last minute when it seemed the little car couldn't possibly hold another person. Mr. Purdy remembered how the crowd at the Garden had roared with glee. He saw, definitely, nothing amusing now.

In the ensuing uproarious reunion, nobody—excepting Sonny—paid any attention as he gathered up the enlarger and scattered negatives. Sonny, a package of the frozen meat clamped in his jaws, trotted after him, leaped on the bed and began chewing the wrapper. Mr. Purdy was too dazed to give more than passing notice; he could simply be thankful he had taken no pictures of the elephants.

Placing the enlarger on a glass-topped table, he rummaged in a drawer. Only Agnes Purdy, he acknowledged with a sense of abject defeat, could cope with this ridiculous situation. And somewhere he had a very good shot of her...

Mrs. Purdy, standing in her characteristic arms-akimbo pose like a general commanding his troops, did not seem at all astonished to find herself in her husband's bedroom. She was only mildly surprised to confront Sonny.

"Morton Purdy!" she exclaimed. "What's that beast doing here? Scat!"

Sonny, having never encountered anyone as formidable as Mrs. Purdy, stopped chewing the wrapper, raised his head, then quickly jumped from the bed and slunk into the hall. Mrs.

Purdy followed with purposeful step. A moment later she was back.

"Morton!" she demanded ominously. "Who are all those people? And what, please, have you been up to?"

With relief and chagrin, Mr. Purdy explained.

"Hmph!" said Mrs. Purdy when she'd sized up the how's and wherefore's. "Any fool can plainly see what to do. Reverse it!"

"What?" said Mr. Purdy.

"Reverse it, you idiot, lens and negative, the whole kit and kaboodle."

Mr. Purdy sat down and reversed the lens. Removing the negative of Mrs. Purdy and absently putting it in his pocket, he inserted with considerable satisfaction, its dull side up, the negative of the detestable Captain Stevens and Sonny. He switched on the enlarger light, stepped into the hall, and peered into the living room uproar. Nothing had happened. Captain Stevens and his beast were still among the roistering present.

Mrs. Purdy's eyes narrowed. "I think this calls for more drastic medicine." She went into the kitchen and returned with a box of matches.

The stuff from which modern photographic negatives are manufactured does not burn easily. But burn it certainly does when a flame is pressed against it. Mrs. Purdy placed the negative of the Captain and Sonny on the glass table top and watched it slowly curl to a bubbly crisp.

One by one Mrs. Purdy relentlessly destroyed the negatives. And when they were all burned, and the house was quiet, and Mr. Purdy was feeling queasy, she turned on her spouse.

"Now you," she barked, "get out of here while I clean up this mess."

"But where should I go?"

"Go down and get yourself a drink," she said. "Get two drinks. Get loaded. But," and she glared at the enlarger, "don't you ever come near this thing again!"

Mr. Purdy was lifting his third beer at Joe's when the televised ball game was suddenly interrupted with a special announcement.

"Boston!" cried the announcer. "Seventeen circus performers were burned to death this afternoon when fire flashed through their dressing rooms. The dead included the world-famous aerialist, Lola Lark. The flames spread to the menagerie and at least one tiger was—"

Mr. Purdy stood paralyzed. As the full import sank in, sweat oozed from his forehead. His eyes glazed. His mouth opened and closed and opened again.

"Joe," he managed weakly. "Joe, I think I need something a little stronger."

"Coming up," said Joe.

Mr. Purdy reached into his pocket for the money. His fingers touched something slick. Fishing it out, he found with fascinated horror that it was the negative of Agnes Purdy. For a long and terribly uncertain moment, Mr. Purdy studied her granite features.

"And Joe," he said at last with calm decision, "let's have a match."

THE END

FIX ME SOMETHING TO EAT

By *William P. McGivern*

How good would your appetite be if you were invited to dinner and found the main course would be yourself?

"WE HAVEN'T got a chance, Barny."

"Shut up! Keep your eye on that cop at the corner."

The two speakers were crouched beside a third floor window overlooking the street. It was nighttime and their shadows loomed intermittently against a wall of the room, appearing and disappearing in unison with the neon sign that flashed from the top of a building across the street.

One of the men was huge and powerful with great broad shoulders and a full strong face. His name was Barny Myers. His eyes, small, cold, expressionless, were a better clue to his character than his open features.

The other man was smaller, plumply built, with soft, almost feminine features and curly blond hair. His pouting lips gave him the look of a sadistic cherub. His name was Filbert Smith and he was nicknamed Filly.

Now he cast a beseeching glance at Barny's grim profile, and said: "They've got us surrounded. The street is too quiet."

"Maybe they have, and maybe they haven't," Barny said. The neon light flashed across his face, brought out the gleam in his eyes and glinted on the gun in his big hand. "They don't know what building we're in, though. If they did we'd have heard from them before this."

"They been clearing people out of the block all day," Filly said. "They're ready to come after us."

"We'll be here when they do," Barny said. "It wouldn't be polite not to welcome the lousy rats. Keep your eye on that cop. He'll probably give the signal."

At the corner of the block a man stood reading the paper. He wore a trench coat with the collar turned up against the misting rain that was falling.

Filly watched this man and the breath was ragged in his throat.

Barny Myers and Filbert Smith had robbed a bank in the center of town the day before and the proceeds of the job—sixty-eight thousand dollars—was securely stacked away in a small black bag in the closet of the room. They had planned to get clear out of the state by this time, but a series of incredibly bad breaks had completely shattered their schedule. First, a nervous guard at the bank had gone for his gun. They had shot him dead, but in the excitement a teller pressed a general alarm that had brought dozens of police cars to the scene. Driving off in the getaway car they had crashed into a milk wagon at the first intersection. They had abandoned the car and stolen another, but within half a mile the engine had sputtered and died. They saw then that the gas gauge read: Empty!

They had set off on foot, dodged through alleys and streets and finally had come across this rooming house. The landlady, a drunken old drudge, had given them a room and they had settled down for a siege.

A GENTLE knock sounded on the door.

Barny wheeled, his lips forming a silent oath.

"It's them!" Filly squealed.

"Shut up!" Barny said. He walked to the door, moving slowly and stealthily, and his gun was ready. Gripping the knob, he turned it slowly, and then jerked open the door.

A small girl with enormous eyes and dark pigtails stood in the corridor. She let out a tiny scream and then clapped both hands over her mouth.

"What'd ya want?" Barny snapped. The girl's eyes were fixed in awe on the gun. She took her hands away from her mouth and whispered, "Is that a real gun? The kind cowboys wear? I saw one in a circus once, only it had a shiny handle."

"What'd ya want?" Barny repeated.

"My mother sent me to get you," the little girl said. "She's sick and she sent me to get somebody to help her. She has to go to the hospital," she added, and her voice was solemn with the importance of her mother's illness.

"Where is your mother?"

"Just down the hall. Will you come and help her?"

There was a speculative light in Barny's tiny eyes. "Yeah, I'll come with you, kid."

"For God's sake!" Filly cried hoarsely.

"Shut up!" Barny said. "Maybe we'll take the kid's mother to a hospital."

"Are you crazy?"

"Think it over, stupe, and you'll get the idea. Come on, kid, take me to your mother."

"Oh, thank you."

Barny followed the little girl down the corridor and turned into a room whose door was standing open. He saw a tired-looking young woman of perhaps twenty-eight or thirty lying in a narrow bed with the covers pulled up to her throat.

"It was good of you to come," she said, smiling weakly at Barny.

"He's going to help you, Mommy," the little girl said.

"What's your trouble?" Barny said.

"I think it might be pneumonia," the woman answered. "I worked late the other night, you see, and got soaked coming home. The next morning after I'd taken Judy to school, I began to feel that I was coming down with something."

"Well, I think the best thing to do is take you to a hospital," Barny said.

"I—I don't have any money. It will have to be the County Hospital."

"Don't you worry about that, just get into some kind of a wrapper and we'll get started."

Barny went back to his own room while the woman was dressing. Filly looked at him and shook his head. "I don't get it."

Barny peered out the window at the cop at the corner. "Still waiting for us, eh?" he said, his voice grin. "Well, they won't have to wait much longer. We're leaving, Filly. We're walking out of here with that brat and her mother as shields."

Filly nodded and smiled slowly. His little mouth looked like a rosy O. "I understand now," he said. "For a minute I thought you might be trying to relive your days in the Boy Scouts."

"They wouldn't let me in the Scouts when I was a kid," Barny said, grinning. "I had a bad reputation on account of blowing the safe at the corner drug store when I was ten years old. Come on. Get the money and let's go."

HE WALKED back to the sick woman's room and helped her to her feet. She was wearing a blue robe and slippers and her face was drawn and pale. "I'm not sure I can make it," she said. "My knees are like water."

"You can make it all right," Barny said. "Try real hard."

They went into the corridor and started down the rickety steps. Barny had his left arm about the woman's waist and his right hand was in his suit coat pocket holding his gun. Filly came after them holding the little girl's hand.

When they reached the first floor hallway Barny jerked his head at Filly. "Check the back entrance."

Filly hurried off and Barny was alone with the woman and her daughter. There was one light in the hallway, a glaring unshaded bulb hanging from the ceiling, and in its pitiless illumination the rugs and furniture and wall paper seemed a bit cheaper than they actually were.

"I don't understand this," the woman said. She was leaning heavily on Barny's arm. "Why are we waiting here?"

"We're going out the back way," Barny said. "Now shut up. I got things on my mind."

"But—"

"I said, shut up."

The little girl began to cry. "Don't you say that to my Mommy."

Filly came back and Barny nodded at the little girl. "Shut her up," he said. "How's the back?"

"Okay. It leads to an alley, which leads to a street. We can get a car there maybe." Filly scooped the little girl up as he was talking and clapped a hand firmly over her mouth. "Follow me," he said. "We won't run into trouble until we hit that street. They'll be waiting there, I guess."

Barny dragged the woman roughly down the corridor and through a kitchen to the backyard. The small party proceeded into the alley and turned to the right. Ahead was a street, and by the light of a lamp at the intersection, Barny saw a parked car with a man sitting behind the wheel. It wasn't a police car, so Barny began to grin. This might solve everything.

Actually it couldn't have been simpler...

There were cops waiting, all right, and they flashed lights on them but held their fire when they saw the hostages. Barny chased the man from the car, which was a big powerful Cadillac, and pushed the woman into the front seat, while Filly was leaping into the back with the child.

Barny gave the car the gun and raced right through the police cordon, and not a shot was fired; but three squad cars set off after them with sirens screaming.

That was when they got their first break in the whole miserable undertaking. Leaving the south end of town barely two blocks ahead of the racing police cars they managed to squeeze through a rail crossing inches ahead of a lumbering freight train. The police cars were blocked and Barny and Filly had the open highway to themselves.

"What about the woman and the kid?" Filly said.

"Toss 'em out. I'll slow down."

"No—no," the woman said, and her voice was barely a whimper.

Barny slowed down to about forty. "Okay, hurry up," he snapped.

Filly opened the door and shoved the wailing child onto the running board. She clung to his arms, sobbing, and he had to strike her across the face to make her let go. The woman was too weak to struggle; but she stared at Barny with eyes that were suddenly murderous with hate.

"God will punish you," she gasped. "He will pay you back for this—this devilishness."

Barny shoved her out of the car with one powerful thrust of his arm and stepped on the accelerator. Filly peered out of the rear window. The child was lying perfectly still in the middle of the road, in a small crumpled heap, and the mother, he saw with astonishment, was trying to crawl toward her daughter. The woman's back or leg was broken because her progress was flopping and uneven, but the fact that she could make the effort at all struck Filly as remarkable.

"This mother love is quite a thing," he said to Barny. And then he grinned because he didn't like or trust any women…

THEY COVERED fifty miles in the next forty-five minutes, and Barny began to scowl.

"We got to get off this road. They've wired ahead probably by now."

"I'll watch for a place to turn off," Filly said.

Ten minutes later he spotted a graveled side road. He shouted and Barny slapped on the brakes, then backed up and turned off onto the side road.

They went on for the next hour or so, following the narrow winding road through country that became increasingly wild and virgin. Tall trees grew up straight from the sides of the road, and between the great trunks there was an almost impenetrable screen of underbrush.

"This is perfect," Barny said, grinning. "I knew there were woods out this way from town but I thought they'd be full of houses and people. But you could lose a whole regiment in here without missing 'em."

Finally the road ended in a small clearing. They climbed out of the car and peered around, somewhat abashed by the deep unmoving silence. The moonlight that filtered through the trees was weak and pale.

"Well, what now?" Filly said, and unconsciously lowered his voice.

"We'll push on into the woods," Barny said. "First, we'll hide the car, though. We can go through these woods and come out on the other side by tomorrow morning. Then we grab another car and keep going."

They drove the car as deep into the bushes as they could and covered it with tree branches. When that was done Filly picked up the satchel of money and followed Barny into the woods...

Six hours later they stopped for about the fifth time to smoke a cigarette and get their breath. They sat on the end of an upturned log and listened to the creepy silence.

"Damn place gets on my nerves," Filly said.

"As long as you don't hear nothing you're okay," Barny said. "Just remember that."

"What do you mean?"

"Dogs. Did you ever have dogs after you?"

"No," Filly said.

"It ain't any fun."

"Well, who'd set dogs after us?" Filly said uneasily.

"The police might. They find that we took to the woods and they'll break out dogs, all right. Let's get moving."

"Sure, what are we waiting for?" Filly said, with a glance over his shoulder.

They kept on the rest of the night and by dawn both men were tired and hungry. It was cold in the woods, a dank clammy wind mourned about them constantly, and they had been unable to find water.

"So we'd be in the clear by morning, eh?" Filly said, sarcastically.

"Shut up!" Barny said. "I didn't know these damn woods were so deep."

"Well, I'm not moving another step until I get good and rested," Filly said, flopping down on the cold hard ground. He closed his eyes and breathed slowly and gratefully.

A sound that was somewhat like the thin wailing of a flute drifted in with the wind.

Barny turned his head sharply, trying to guess its direction.

"What's that?" Filly said.

"Dogs, bloodhounds. You can stay and get a good rest if you want," he said with harsh cruelty and strode off into the trees.

"Barney, wait for me," Filly cried, scrambling to his feet...

THE NOISE of the dogs grew in volume with every mile they covered. They were running now, stumbling occasionally in the heavy brush, but recovering as quickly as they could and staggering on to keep ahead of the devil-sound that whined in the wind.

Finally, Barny stopped and listened a moment. They could still hear the dogs, but the sound was fainter now.

"They lose the trail?" Filly said, and the words came out like sobs.

"No, they've stopped. It ain't right. I know dogs and they don't stop like that."

"What'll we do?"

"Keep going!"

They plunged on into the brush, too tired to notice the branches that lashed their faces, even too tired to feel the terrible pangs of hunger and thirst. Then they heard a new sound before them, a chopping noise, the unmistakable sound of an axe biting into wood.

Barny took the gun from his pocket and moved ahead cautiously toward that familiar sound. He pulled a heavy bush aside and peered into a clearing.

There an old man was chopping wood. He was a fat little man with silvery hair and a tiny gray beard. He wore a soft flannel shirt and baggy trousers and he was humming a tune under his breath as he swung the axe with inefficient gusto at the log between his feet.

Barny dropped the gun slowly back into his pocket and winked at Filly. Then he pushed the brush aside and stepped into the clearing.

"Howdy, Pop," he said.

The old man looked up with a surprised smile on his face. He studied Filly and Barny for a second or two, and it was obvious that his old brain was struggling to assess the situation. Then he said: "'Allo, my friends."

"Our car broke down and we're looking for some place to get some food and a bed," Barny said. "Can you help us out?"

"Oh, yes, yes," the old man said eagerly. There was something foreign about his accent. It sounded faintly French, Filly decided. "You come with me. You are tired, *non?* And hungry, eh? We will fix all of that."

"Who's 'we?'" Barny said, and then his hand started moving unconsciously to his pocket.

"My wife Marie." He laughed and the wrinkles about his eyes puckered in dozens of wreaths and crisscrosses. "She is good cook, you'll see. You come, eh?"

"Sure," Barny said. He laughed shortly. "We'll come."

The old man led them about a half mile along a faintly marked trail and when they turned sharply for about the twentieth time they saw a weather-beaten frame house set in the middle of a clearing. There was a barn and several outbuildings clustered about it, and chickens and dogs were running about in the hard-packed dirt yard.

"You don't have many people come this way, I'll bet," Barny said.

"No, nobody comes here anymore," the old man said. "Long time ago, when we first arrive, many people used to come by. But times change, people grow old..." He sighed and left the sentence unfinished.

THE OLD MAN'S feminine counterpart appeared on the porch and shouted a cheery hallo at them. She was short and dumpy with plump rosy cheeks and white hair tied in a bun at the base of her neck. An enormous apron covered her ample waist and fell clear to the tips of her brightly polished shoes.

"This is Mama," the old man said, smiling at her with pleasure. "Mama, these good men need food and a bed."

"Were they in an accident?" Mama said. "There is blood on their faces." Her eyes were very dark and solicitous and she ran the tip of a tiny tongue over her full lips in a gesture of anxiety.

"Now do not jabber like a bird," the old man said, but his voice was kind. "We will take care of them first, and let them tell us about themselves later."

"Yes, Papa," the little woman said, and hurried off.

Papa took them into the warm comfortably furnished parlor and with much bustling and muttering under his breath found glasses and poured them each a generous portion of brandy. After that he led them upstairs to a bedroom where Mama was filling basins with hot water. Soap and towels were ready for their use, and Papa brought them two old flannel shirts from his room.

"Maybe they are too leetle, eh? But they are clean, *non?*"

With that he left them alone.

Barny looked at Filly, a slow grin spreading across his face. "I think we hit a perfect spot," he said. "There's no radio or telephone here, and these old duffers will put us up forever. Perfect, eh?"

Filly grinned too and stripped off his shirt...

Downstairs, half an hour later, they found an amazing breakfast waiting for them. Chicken livers, broiled to tender succulence in a sauce of wine and oil, golden potatoes swimming in butter graced with chives and garlic, a platter of rosy-yoked eggs, rich yellow muffins—Barny and Filly hardly knew where to start. There were flagons of rich Burgundy to wash down the food and steaming hot coffee to chase the wine.

Afterward Mama brought in a plum pudding steeped in brandy and a plate of sharp cheeses.

"Now you sleep good, eh?" Papa said, twinkling at them over his spectacles.

"Brother, what food!" Barny said, letting out his breath reverently. "How about you? Aren't you eating?"

"Oh, I've had my breakfast," Papa said.

"And Mama?"

"Yes, Mama too. We just enjoy watching you eat. Eh, Mama?"

Mama blushed and laughed, and Filly, who was oddly perceptive about relationships between men and women, guessed that Papa's remark was a private joke, and probably a slightly off-color one.

The two men ate and drank the rich heavy food and wine until their eyelids began to droop from exhaustion. Then Papa led them to their bedroom, turned down the covers and opened the window. "Now you get good sleep, eh?"

Barny and Filly stretched out on the bed and were both asleep before the old man tiptoed from the room...

WHEN THEY awoke it was dark and the wind that blew in the open window was cold and sharp. Filly got up and lighted a candle on the dresser and closed the window.

"It's damn odd, but I'm hungry," he said. "After that breakfast I didn't think I could eat for a week. But I feel like I'm starving. I hope supper's as good as that first meal was."

"Well, let's find out. I guess we wore ourselves out in that hike. I'm weak as a cat."

Mama and Papa were sitting in the parlor, but jumped up when the two men came in. "I was just to call you," Mama said gaily. "Dinner is all ready."

"Great!" Barny said.

"Perhaps a leetle drink first for the appetite?" Papa said, smiling like a man of the world.

Dinner was a replica of breakfast as far as bounty was concerned. There were two roasts, dripping with blood-red gravy, a variety of vegetables, each with its own rich sauces, and breads, cakes, puddings, and cheeses in profligate abundance.

Barny and Filly were halfway through their first heaping platefuls when they noticed that Mama and Papa were not eating.

"Hey, you don't know what you're missing," Barny said. He, himself, felt that he couldn't get enough of the rich spicy food. Every nerve and muscle in his body seemed to be crying for replenishment.

"Mama and I ate earlier," Papa said, and again, Filly noticed, Mama put her head back and laughed, while a warm rush of color stained her plump cheeks.

After dinner they sat in the parlor and sipped brandy. A fire glowed in the hearth and the only sound was the pleasant sighing of the wind against the windowpanes.

"It's nice and quiet here," Barny said. He looked from Mama to Papa, "You like that, eh?"

"Oh, yes, we like it nice and quiet," Papa said.

"Nobody ever comes by for any reason?" Filly asked.

"But hardly ever," Mama said.

Barny's eyes drooped sleepily. With an effort he forced them open. "We thought we heard some dogs when we were out in the woods," he said.

"Well, we have dogs," Papa said, smiling.

"No, these were off in the other direction."

"I did not hear them," Papa said. His smile became apologetic. "But my ears are getting old, eh? They do not hear everything so good anymore."

Suddenly, unmistakably, an automobile horn blasted the silence.

Barny came to his feet in a crouch. "Nobody comes by here, eh?" he said harshly to Papa.

"But who can it be?" Papa said.

"I got a hunch you know."

Mama got to her feet and stood wringing her hands. "Do not be upset. Papa will send whoever it is away. We have known persecution too. Think of us as your friends. You are in trouble, eh?"

"Yeah, and that means you're in trouble too," Barny said. "You and Kris Kringle here. If he doesn't get rid of whoever's heading this way you'll both learn what trouble is."

Papa got to his feet with perfect composure and slipped into a leather jacket. "You go into the kitchen," he said to Barny and Filly.

"Okay, but one funny move will be your last, remember that."

Barny stepped into the kitchen and walked to the window. Filly was at his side and both men had their guns in their hands.

THEY LOOKED out into the moonlit yard and saw half a dozen men walking toward the house. The men carried rifles in the crooks of their arms and behind them, at least a hundred yards back, were the lights of a small truck.

"How'd they get that in here?" Filly said.

"Must be another route."

The men stopped about fifteen yards from the house. Barny heard the front door slam, then Papa's voice: "'Allo there, my friends. What you want?"

One of the men called out: "This is Sheriff Watson. You see a couple of men around here today, Mister Saint Gwynn." He pronounced the name: Sang Gwine.

"But *non*, my friends."

"You sure?"

"But of course." Papa laughed cheerfully. "You come in and look around, eh?"

Some of the men moved back toward the car, Barny noticed. Sheriff Watson said, "No, that won't be necessary," and Papa laughed again, good-naturedly.

The group drifted back to the car and Barny heard the motor start. The car moved away and soon its noise was swallowed up by the night.

Putting their guns away, Barny and Filly walked back into the living room. Papa was removing his jacket, a triumphant little grin on his face.

"You see, my friends," he said, studying them with his cheery twinkling eyes. "They believe me when I tell them I see no one."

Barney sat down in a comfortable chair and scowled at the fire. Several things were bothering him. "That's a queer sheriff," he said, at last. "He didn't even search the house. I wish all cops were that dumb."

"Or that scared," Filly said. Things were bothering Filly too. He had noticed the reluctance of the sheriff's men, and the nervous way they had peered about them while the sheriff was talking with Papa.

"What were they scared of?" Barny said to Filly.

Filly shrugged. "Maybe Papa knows."

Papa spread his hands in a gesture of bewilderment, but Mama suddenly put her knitting aside firmly. "You are right, they are afraid of us," she said. "Ever since we come from old country the people around here are afraid of us. They are—how-you-say—superstitious."

"Mama is telling the truth," Papa said sadly. "You know how it is? We have other customs, other ways of speaking, and our neighbors regard that as something *terrible.*"

"It started in the war," Mama said excitedly. "When the fighting was going on near here and we went out to help the wounded." She wet her red lips nervously. "They would not even let us do that."

"Well, we are used to it now," Papa said. He patted his wife's hand gently. "Let us try to forget, eh?"

Barny yawned. He couldn't keep his mind on the conversation. Every inch of him ached with weariness. "I'm going to get some sleep, if you folks will excuse me," he muttered.

"But of course. And sleep well. No one will disturb you," Papa said.

UPSTAIRS, Filly sat on the edge of the wide bed and stared at the floor with a petulant frown. "Barny," he said, at last, "this is the country they fought the Civil War in, that's right, isn't it?"

"That's right. Part of it, anyway," Barny said, stretching out on the bed without bothering to remove his clothes.

Filly turned to him anxiously. "Well, you heard what Mama said, didn't you? That they tried to help the wounded when the fighting was going on? She must have meant the Civil War."

"Ah, she's cracked," Barny mumbled sleepily. "Hell, she wasn't even born when the Civil War started. That was all of ninety years ago."

"What was she talking about then?"

"I tell you she's cracked," Barny said. "Shut up and lemme get some sleep."

"I don't like it here, Barny."

But Barny was fast asleep. Filly stared at him angrily for a few seconds; but then his own eyes began to droop and he was suddenly overcome with drowsiness. Resolving to discuss the matter in the morning he lay down beside Barny and almost instantly fell asleep...

The next morning both men were refreshed and cheerful. Barny ran his hands through his thick hair and then flexed his arms. "I feel like a new man," he announced happily. He scratched his three-day beard. "I'll grab a shave before breakfast. You need one too, Filly. We stumbled into luck when we hit this place, I tell you."

"I suppose so," Filly said. He remembered his anxiety of last night, but it seemed ludicrous in the clean bright sunlight that spilled into the room. From downstairs they could hear Mama bustling about in the kitchen and the aroma of broiling liver and bacon drifted up to them and set their mouths watering.

Papa came in a few seconds later carrying a tray on which there were two mugs of coffee and a plate of hot buttered biscuits. "Always before breakfast there is the little coffee and a bun," he said, beaming at them. "It is a custom in my country."

"Great," Barny said. "It's a wonderful custom."

"Where is your country, by the way?" Filly said.

"Austria," Papa said.

"Say, how about borrowing a razor," Barny said. "We'll look human after a shave."

"But of course."

Papa hurried out and returned a few minutes later with two clean straight razors, soap mugs and towels; but he had forgot a mirror. Barny asked him about it, but Papa said apologetically that there wasn't a mirror in the house. Then Filly remembered that he had a small one in his wallet. He dug his wallet out of his coat and went through it carefully but the mirror was gone.

He stood in the middle of the room with the wallet in his hand and suddenly he felt cold and afraid. Papa was smiling at him and Barny was testing the razor on his thumb. Filly didn't know why he was afraid; but from some depth in his subconscious he could feel a faint memory of horror roiling and twisting.

"It is lost?" Papa asked.

"Yes, I guess so," Filly said; he shivered.

"Well, I can get by without a mirror," Barny said. "I know where my face is, I guess."

"Good. I will wait for you downstairs," Papa said and left the room.

Filly shaved in silence. He cut himself once but it was only a nick.

When he was through he cleaned the razor carefully and then dried his face. Barny inspected him critically. "Just a couple of cuts, which isn't too bad without a mirror," he said.

"A couple of cuts?"

"Yeah, one on your cheek, and one on your throat."

Filly's hand touched his neck, his fingers moved about gently. He felt a tiny opening just beside his adam's apple. "I didn't cut myself there," he said slowly.

"Well, maybe it's a mosquito bite." Filly looked at Barny sharply. He saw a tiny cut on Barny's throat. "You nicked yourself too," he said.

"I did not," Barny said. He felt the scratch and frowned. "Maybe a mosquito got me too," he said. "Come on, let's go down to breakfast. I'm starved again."

"So am I," Filly said. "I wish I wasn't."

"Don't be a fool. We're lucky to have good appetites considering the food Mama dishes out."

Filly hesitated a moment; and then he sighed and followed Barny downstairs...

THE DAYS sped by quickly. Barny and Filly fell into an unvarying routine of eating and drinking and sleeping. They were always tired, always hungry, always thirsty. It got to be too much trouble to stay up during the days, so they lay on their bed most of the time napping, and not even bothering to talk to each other.

One day Filly noticed that his clothes were hanging loosely on him. For all the rich food he was eating he was losing weight! He glanced at Barny, seeing him it seemed for the first time in weeks, and he was amazed to note that the once huge man was a hulk of his former self.

Barny's shirt hung like a tent over his bony shoulders and his cheeks were sunken and drawn.

"Barny, something's wrong with us," Filly said in a weak voice. "We're fading away, dying."

But Barny only grunted and slumped onto the bed. "I'm hungry," he muttered. "Hungry."

"But we just ate."

"I'm always hungry."

Filly stared at Barny's recumbent form for a moment or two; and then he made a decision. Turning away, he walked downstairs. Mama and Papa were sitting in the living room. Mama was knitting, and Papa was staring into the fire with a faint smile on his face. He looked up at Filly. "Ah, hello there, my friend," he said.

"I'm going for a walk," Filly said. He watched them, swaying slightly on his feet, convinced that they would prevent him from leaving in some manner. But Papa nodded approvingly. "That is good idea," he said. "Walking makes the appetite, eh?"

Filly made a strangling sound in his throat and hurried out the door. When he was across the clearing and into the sheltering woods he began to run with frantic, hysterical speed. The trailing vines snapped at his face and his body, and occasionally he tripped over a root and fell headlong. But he fought on as if all the devils in hell were at his heels.

How long he ran he had no way of knowing. But at last he was forced to stop. Sobbing for breath he sat on a log and tried to muster the strength to keep going. But he was empty, drained. His strength was gone. He slipped from the log and lay flat on his back staring at the blue sky.

Night settled slowly over the forest. Filly fell asleep several times. Each time he woke he felt the coldness in his body and he knew that if he didn't rouse himself he would die.

Summoning his last bit of energy he forced himself to his feet. Tottering weakly he tried to plot a course; but he knew nothing about the stars or the woods. He began co cry. The tears ran down his thin cheeks and were frozen by the whipping wind. A bird screamed above him and Filly started in terror.

"I must go back," he whispered to the darkness. Barny was there; he could protect him. Hunger was growing in him like an aching physical thing. Turning he trudged weakly back toward Mama and Papa's farmhouse.

The cheery lights of the front room showed up through the trees in a manner of minutes; and he realized with despair that he had only gone about a hundred yards in a wild dash to freedom.

MAMA AND Papa met him at the front door with bustling solicitude.

"We thought you were lost," Papa said, helping him to a chair. "Some brandy, eh? You are cold, *non?*"

"I will fix your dinner," Mama said, and flitted off to the kitchen.

"No, no food," Filly gasped. "Where is Barny?"

"He is gone," Papa said.

"Gone?" The words were only a whisper. He stared up at Papa's round beaming face. "Gone where? Where did he go?"

Papa shrugged. "He said he must leave. That is all I know."

"No, no," Filly cried.

"You are tired," Papa said gently. "You must eat something and rest, eh?"

Mama came in with a tray of food.

There was a whole chicken, steaming in a gravy of wine and blood, and a flagon of rich red wine.

"This will do you good, eh?" She said. She licked her lips and looked down on him with a smile. "You must get your strength back," she said.

"Get it back so you can take it away?"

The thought hammered in Filly's mind. He tried to lift himself from the chair but his arms had no strength. Papa cut a sliver of meat from the breast of the chicken and gently put it between Filly's lips. "You must eat," he said in a low crooning voice.

The taste of the food inflamed Filly. His hunger was suddenly wild and frantic. He tore at the chicken and wolfed down large pieces of the succulent meat. Papa poured wine for him, which he gulped with desperate haste. Finally, sated and groggy, he slumped back in the chair, feeling his strength returning slowly.

Mama and Papa watched him approvingly.

"Now you must sleep," Mama said in a firm maternal voice.

"Yes, I must sleep," Filly said; but his brain was plotting warily.

He got to his feet and went up the stairs to his bedroom. Inside he closed the door and hurried to the closet where he kept his gun. It was still there, hanging on a peg. He jerked it from the holster and stuck it in the waistband of his trousers. And then, as he was starting to close the door, he saw the black bag in which they had kept their money.

He sank to his knees and opened it with trembling fingers. The money was still there, in sheafs of neat banknotes.

Filly knew then that Barny hadn't gone away. He wouldn't have left without the money.

FILLY GOT slowly to his feet and backed away from the bag of money as if it were an object of horror. He thought someone was in the room with him, heard someone hammering a blunt object against the walls; but then he knew that it was only his own heartbeat he was hearing.

He turned the knob of the door slowly and stepped out into the dark corridor. From below a wavering flash of firelight touched the stairs; and he could hear Mama and Papa talking.

"You are always so greedy, Mama." Papa's voice was fond, almost endearing.

"Oh, let's hurry," Mama said. Her voice was excited as a schoolgirl's. "He must be asleep by now."

"Now, now, we must be patient. You shouldn't have gone to the other one this afternoon. He was too weak. Now he is gone forever. All because my little girl is too greedy."

"He was about all done anyway. Come, Papa, let us go up for the other one. It has been so long since we've had visitors."

"Very well," Papa said indulgently.

Filly backed into his room, closing the door with clammy twitching fingers.

"God, God," he moaned, but the words stuck in his throat and he nearly vomited.

He heard light footsteps on the stairs.

He hurled himself on the bed, pulled the gun from his waist.

The footsteps approached his room, and then the door swung inward with a gentle protesting creak.

He saw them framed in the flickering shadowy firelight, saw their silvery heads, their placid contented features, their dumpy peasant's bodies. And he knew *what* they were.

"Stop!" he cried hoarsely.

They paid no attention to his words. They came into the room and moved slowly toward the bed.

Filly fired six shots at them, as fast as finger could work trigger. The butt of the gun slammed into the heel of his palm, and the shots echoed bangingly in the tiny room. Cordite soured the air.

Filly blinked and then screamed.

Mama and Papa were still walking toward him, and they were smiling eagerly now. The moonlight touched their glistening red lips and sharp white teeth.

Filly tried again to scream but the muscles of his throat were paralyzed.

And then they were on him; and in the brief moments left to him he learned that the reality was incredibly more monstrous than he had feared it would be.

THE END

ACCORDING TO PLAN

By Jack Sharkey

The blonde looked as if her touch would be the greatest pleasure. Instead it was just the opposite.

CAREY PHILIPS would probably have given the blonde only a minor survey as he moved to the rear of the bus, except that she was a brunette. Although he normally preferred a seat beside the window, and there were two vacant behind where she was sitting, he sat down beside her, instead, and took another look at her hair while pretending to observe people passing on the sidewalk.

It was true. Her long dark hair had short yellow roots. Carey was properly amazed. He'd seen many a *reverse* case, of course, but this was a new twist. And Carey was a news reporter, so—

"I beg your pardon..." he said haltingly.

Warm, startled blue eyes were suddenly looking into his, and Carey flashed a lopsided grin at her, one he'd used to advantage on many occasions. This time, however, it didn't seem to take.

"Oh, no," she said, in a small, weak voice. "You're Carey Philips!" Her face was suddenly intensely pale. Before he could even wonder how she knew—his column carried a by-line, but no picture—she added, "But you're on the wrong bus!"

"I'm on the—?" he blurted, bewildered, then looked at the reverse side of the canvas roll above the windshield at the front of the bus. "I'll be damned. You're right!" he said. "But how—?"

"Oh, this is terrible," she said, nervously. "My first month on the job, too. We— We're not even supposed to meet for another four months...I'd better get off."

"Whoa, there, young lady," Carey said, hastily enclosing her upper arm within his fingers as she tried to get up and past him. "How do you know who I am? Or that I got the wrong bus by mistake, or—" She pulled free of his grasp, then slumped back, abruptly.

"You won't believe me," she sighed. Carey thought he sensed a faint trace of relief in the sigh, as though she were suddenly realizing with considerable happiness that she was safe from some sort of exposure.

"I might," he said. "Go ahead and tell me."

She glanced around a moment, as if ascertaining that she was not being observed then faced him, her tiny heart-shaped face almost laughably solemn. "I think I *will*," she said, coming to a decision. "But please be careful you don't touch me."

"Lady, I assure you my intentions are—"

"No, no, no," she whispered, exasperated. "I didn't mean that sort of thing at all! I mean be careful not to come into contact with me at all. It's—It's fatal. That's why I'm wearing gloves."

A psycho! thought Carey, disappointed. But what the hell, it might make a nice filler for a column that was pretty skimpy otherwise. "Really?" he said, feigning acute credibility on his face. "How does it work? Electric shock, or what?"

"It won't work at all, unless you're on my list," she said, with a tiny smile. "You see that woman up near the front, standing?"

Carey looked. Up front, before the three-seater that ran lengthwise over the wheel, there was a middle-aged woman, hanging onto a strap and conversing rapidly, with a lot of chuckles, with another woman, seated there. Not especially distinguished, either. Green cloth coat, pink hat with rosebuds on it, and a shopping bag dangling from one freckled hand. Hair gray, face a little tired-looking. That was all.

Carey turned back to the girl beside him.

"I see her, yes. What about her?"

"She's going to die, today," said the girl. "I managed to touch her earlier, when the bus was crowded. She never noticed. It's always easier in crowds."

Despite himself, Carey shivered. Psycho she might be, but her cold-blooded pronouncement gave him goosebumps. "Uh—" he said, stuck for a casual comeback, "you just—uh—hanging around to be in on the *fun,* or what?"

"Oh, I wouldn't do that," the girl assured him. "I'd just as soon not be around when it happens. It's just that this is the bus I usually take home, so I just stayed on after—after my work was done." Her voice dropped on the last phrase, guiltily.

"I sense that you don't like your work," Carey remarked dryly.

She made a wry face. "It's not so bad. As long as I don't have to watch, I mean. After all, *someone* has to do it, so it may as well be me." She smiled brightly as she finished.

"Excuse my idiotic non-comprehension, but— Someone has to do *what?"* said Carey, frowning.

"Mark the diers," said the girl. "Otherwise their protective aura would keep them away from harm."

"Oh. Oh, yeah, the protective aura," Carey grunted.

Poor kid. Crazy as a quilt.

There was still a point that had him bothered, though. "Would you mind telling me why you've dyed your hair from blonde?" he said. "If you'll excuse the impertinence?"

She flushed a dull crimson. "I did it myself. I didn't think anyone would notice. It's the attitudes, that's all. That lady up front, she resents blondes. Thinks they're all hussies, or something. She'd have noticed me right away. So I tinted my hair darker, so she wouldn't give me a second glance. For you, in four months' time, I would have been a blonde."

"But I *notice* blondes," said Carey. "Most men do."

Her smile was shyly embarrassed. "With men, we work it in reverse. Men *like* being touched by women."

Some part of Carey's mind suddenly played back her prior statement, and he detected an odd note. "Just a second; you say

you *would* have been a blonde in four months' time for me…
Now what'll you be?"

"Why— It won't be *me* at all," she said. "We'll have to send
another agent. Possibly a dog. Men love to pet dogs—Oh, but
I'm telling you much too much. You shouldn't know anything."

Carey stared at her a moment, then, on an impulse, gripped
the sleeve of her dress near the wrist, and tugged down the back
of her glove with thumb and forefinger of the other hand. She
struggled to get free, but did it quietly, not making any
commotion noticeable to anyone but Carey.

"What are you trying to do?" she said, between clenched
teeth, her arm straining against his superior strength.

"In drug addiction," he said, gently, "they call it the Cold
Turkey cure. I'm just going to touch you, and not die, and
maybe then you and I can go have a talk with this medical friend
of mine, and—"

"You think I'm crazy?" she said, then laughed, suddenly and
without amusement, that brief, harsh expulsion of breath that
comes with abrupt despair. "But Mister Philips, I'll—*Oh!*"

Carey's index finger was lying lightly upon the back of her
hand, and his smile was warm and friendly. "See?" he said.
"No ill effects. I feel just great."

"Of *course* you do!" she said, suddenly bursting into tears.
"I'm not with Disease. I'm with *Violence!*"

Carey blinked. "What are you talking about?"

"Within seven days, now, you'll die a death of violence," she
sobbed, softly. "It wasn't supposed to happen for four
months."

"Easy, honey, easy," Carey said. His heart went out to her.
She was young, pretty, and awfully helpless, even if she was a
screwball. "Don't waste your tears on me. I was a lecherous
old reprobate, anyhow."

"*What?*" she said, staring at him through her sparkling tears.
"I'm not crying over *you!*" Angrily, she got up and squeezed

past him to the aisle, jerking her arm free of his attempted grip. "I'm crying because I may very well lose my *job* over this!"

The bus shuddered to a stop beside the curb, and the girl was down the step and out onto the sidewalk almost before Carey had the sense to descend after her.

"Hold on, there," he said, catching up to her as she strode sniffling along the sidewalk, dodging in and out of the people who flocked in and out of a string of stores. "Wait a minute, can't you?"

She spun about to face him. "All right, what?" she snapped.

Carey grinned. "I thought the least you could do is tell me how it's going to happen, so I can prepare myself…"

"You can't prepare," she said simply, her eyes cold. "It's contrary to the regulations. When death comes to you, it will come from that quarter from which you *least* expect it."

"Oh, now look, lady—" Carey began, but was interrupted by a shrill scream of terror, further up the block. He swung himself about, and looked toward the sound, which was cut off in mid-cry.

At the side of the bus, a crowd of people was gathering, all looking down with horror at something in the street. Carey took in the tableau in an instant, without even moving from where he stood. Someone had been getting off the bus at the next corner, and a car had been coming up beside it. They'd stepped right in front of it.

Between the legs of the gathering crowd, Carey could make out just two things. The victim was wearing a green cloth coat, and the impact of the car had knocked a parcel from her hand to burst open upon the sidewalk: a shopping bag.

"Hell—" Carey gasped, and looked back around to see how the girl was taking the accident. His heart turned to a lump of ice. The brunette-blonde was gone.

"Of *course* it's nonsense, Carey," said Doctor McCleod, shaking his head sagely. "You should have come to me the minute you knew you believed even a *little* of the girl's fantastic story. If you could *see* yourself—I tell you, Carey, if a man came to *you* with a story like this, you'd slip him a fiver for a bottle of scotch, and tell him to forget it the *easy* way."

"But," Carey got out of McCleod's armchair before the desk, and started to pace back and forth on the thick carpet, "I can't forget it, Pete! It couldn't have been a coincidence, happening like that. Two days ago, only! It feels like I've been awake for a *week!* It's that where-you-least-expect-it part that's got me all unstrung. I've suddenly gotten afraid of crossing the streets, even *with* the lights, and elevators give me palpitations. You know," he added, with a short nervous laugh, "I *walked* up here, to your office. Seven floors!"

"You might have had heart failure," McCleod remarked, with a frown.

"Unh-uh," Carey shook his head. "That's not violence, Pete."

"Take it from me, there's nothing very *serene* about a heart attack, pal," McCleod said. Then, as the corners of Carey's mouth tightened and grew pale, he added, "But maybe you're right. It doesn't correspond to our notion of violence. Okay, so you don't cross streets, and don't ride elevators. So what? You can still get beaned by falling plaster, or some secretary at the newspaper accidentally runs you through with a letter-opener... Sorry, Carey, I guess I shouldn't have said that. Maybe you'd better sit down—"

Carey, his face wet and colorless, sank back into the armchair, his fingers gripping the ends of the wooden arms tightly. Then, all at once, his face went slack, and his eyes widened.

"Think of something?" said McCleod, quickly.

"Yeah," said Carey, swinging his gaze to meet the other man's. "Yeah, I just thought of something all right! She said where I least expect it, didn't she? So what if I keep on *expecting* it for these next five days? Where is she *then!?*"

"I don't know where *she* will be," McCleod snorted, "but I know where *you'll* be: In a straitjacket, making burbling noises and rolling your eyes at padded walls! Do you realize you could drive yourself crazy, trying to think of all the possible ways there are to die, Carey? Listen, chum, I'm a doctor, and it's a constant wonder to me that *everybody* isn't dead, what with all the things that can stop a life. There are bloodclots, brain hemorrhages, lung paralysis, and shock. Plain, good, old-fashioned shock. A nice one-syllable term for malfunction of just about everything, simultaneously, about which the medical profession knows less than it cares to admit. And that's only inside you. From the outside, we have germs, poisons, collision, puncture, heat, cold, gas, concussion— Good grief, Carey, what in the name of sanity are you *grinning* about?"

"You forget one thing, Pete," Carey said happily, some of the color returning to his cheeks. "As long as I can think of all the possibilities, and figure they're probably due to happen to me, I *won't* go nuts. What's there to *scare* me? As long as I *expect* something horrible to happen, it *won't*, see? Do you realize that for the next five days, I can be *careless* with my life?"

"Oh, just a minute, boy, that's dangerous, thinking that way," McCleod said, scowling. "You'll walk blithely into the front of a burning ammunition dump, or something. My advice to you is to let me get you admitted to a nice rest home for the remainder of your death-week, and—"

"And on the first night I break my neck falling out of bed! No thanks, Pete. I think my way's better. Hell, this is the opportunity of a lifetime, for a reporter! I can get away with *anything* for these next five days, don't you see?"

Carey was on his feet and headed for the door. McCleod, after a fractional second of indecision, slid open the top drawer of his desk and took out a pistol. *"Carey!"* he said loudly.

Carey turned around, saw the gun, and laughed. "Ah-ah," he shook his head. "Shouldn't have told me. Now I'll be expecting it!"

"Look, Carey," McCleod's face was pained, "I hate to resort to this, but you're not well. You need medical care— Damn it, keep back, will you!" he said, angrily, as Carey advanced upon him with a nonchalant grin.

"You wouldn't use that on me, Pete," Carey said, taking the gun from McCleod's fingers without any trouble whatsoever. "You're only bluffing. But I'd use it on me, because I'm *expecting* it to blow my brains out."

With that, Carey placed the muzzle against his right temple and jerked the trigger three times. The gun clicked harmlessly, and he tossed it down on McCleod's desktop. "See?" he said.

"W-What the hell—?" said McCleod, picking it up. He pointed it at the wall and tugged the trigger. The muzzle spurted flame and there was a loud *Blam!* as the bullet tore a black hole in the pastel plaster of the wall. McCleod swore. "The *Safety* was on!"

"Be seeing you, Pete," said Carey, and he turned and left the office, passing the startled receptionist, about to enter to find the source of the gunshot.

McCleod sat there for only a moment, then he was up and moving after Carey, fast. "Hold it, buddy," he said, in the outer office. "This may make medical history. The least you can do is have a qualified eye-witness along." McCleod's receptionist just stared.

"And again," grinned Carey, "if it *doesn't,* I'll *need* a medic."

"You know," said McCleod, sipping at his highball, "it's beginning to make sense, Carey."

They were in a booth in a small plush bar, in the downtown area that housed both their places of business, on their fourth round of drinks. Carey's face was flushed and happy.

"Sure it does," he said, a little fuzzily. "Like what you were saying, about all the funny little things that can go *phfft* and knock people off. Why *don't* they then, more often-like? I'll tell you why. Because the *aura's* working, that's why they don't."

"That protective aura the girl mentioned?" McCleod asked.

180

"Uh-huh," Carey nodded. "It figures, don't it—Doesn't it, I mean? Like you said, how come *everybody* isn't lying around dead, with all the gizmos that can go out of whack?"

"I dunno," said McCleod, adding for clarity, "I dunno at all."

"Why don't we—" Carey said, then paused to drain his glass, the ice-cubes bumping him on the nose. He waved at the waiter for another one, then turned his bleary eyes back to McCleod's. "Why don't we *prove* it, Pete?"

McCleod focused his eyes on Carey's face with an effort, and said, scowling mightily. "Why don't we prove what?"

"That it's bunk, all of it. Dying, I mean. You gotta be *touched*, see? Otherwise the aura keeps you okay, right?"

"I—I guess so," McCleod said, uncertainly. "But whatta ya mean, *prove* it? Whadda we *do?*"

"We endangerize me, see?" Carey said, his eyes aglow. "And every time nothin' happens, you—you write it down, see? And all at once, we're rish—" He ran his tongue between upper teeth and lip. "—*rich.* See?"

"How?"

"How what?"

"Rish?"

"Uh— We *sell* the story to the paper."

"They won't believe it. Will they?"

"*Sure* they will, on—on accounta I can *prove* it's th'truth."

"Oh, yeah," McCleod nodded. Then, "*How'll* you prove it?"

"By being *'live!'* Carey grinned. "See?"

"S'a wonderful plan!" McCleod nodded, looking up and blinking as the waiter brought the fresh round of drinks and took the empty glasses away. "Wonderful," he repeated. "Well, here's to ya."

"Yeah."

They clicked glasses, drained the contents, and left the bar, walking steadily, maybe a little too steadily, out into the warm October night. The street outside was more or less deserted, the nearest people being at a distant corner.

"Where to?" said McCleod, swaying a bit as they came to a sudden standstill at the curb.

"To danger," said Carey. "A fire, or a holdup, or—"

"I don't see any fire, nowheres," McCleod complained, bitterly.

"We could start one—" Carey said brightly, then frowned. "But someone *else* might get hurt, only."

"Yeah," McCleod agreed. "Yeah. What *we* need… What we really *need*, my friend, is a *singular*-type danger, for you only."

"Swell! …What?" said Carey.

"Well—I could push you down a manhole," McCleod offered.

"Nope. You can't."

"Why not?"

"On accounta *you* gotta be writin' everything *down*, see?"

"Uh—Oh, yeah, I forgot. Okay, *what*, then?"

Carey crinkled up his forehead in a massive scowl, and thought very hard. Then he grinned, like a small boy. "Th'zoo! We let ourselves into the lions cage at th'*zoo!*"

"Hey, that's a wonderful—   *We?*" McCleod croaked, abruptly.

"You gotta write it down, don'tcha?" Carey insisted.

McCleod thought it over. "I can write better *outside* the cage," he said suddenly.

"How do ya know? Ever *tried* inside?"

"Mmmm— No. It's—It's just a *feeling* I have, is all."

Carey shrugged. "Okay… But stand close, so you don't *miss* nothing. *Hey! Cab!*"

In the cab beside his friend, who was breathing deeply and nasally, almost asleep with the alcohol in his system, McCleod leaned back and let the cool breeze through the half-open window fan some of the fever from his cheek. A certain consciousness of incongruity in his and his companion's behavior was becoming apparent to him as they rode, and he found himself bothered by it. His partial stupor had all but vanished during the ride.

"Carey..." he said, suddenly leaning forward, the better to turn his head and face his friend. "I wonder if we're behaving quite rationally?"

Carey's lashes fluttered, and he blinked himself to alertness. "How do you mean, Pete?" he said, squinting in a vain attempt to discern the other's features in the intermittent light that fell within the vehicle from passing street lamps. "We're not drunk, if that's what you mean. Just a little woozy, maybe..."

"Exactly," McCleod nodded, worried. "I feel like a pawn in a colossal chess game, all at once. I'm a doctor, Carey, and supposed by most people to be more than normally rational, yet instead of sending for the police when you fled from my office, I came along *with* you. And now, I realize I've agreed to help you into the lion's cage at the zoo! It can't be the drinks. I've had lots more than that and remained quite clear-headed. There's something else."

"What?" Carey said, much of the furry sibilance leaving his tongue. "You don't think we're playing into their hands, maybe?"

"I don't know," said McCleod, sincerely. "But I know that what we're setting out to do is insane."

Carey ran his tongue over dry lips, and considered. "Pete— You're right! It *is* nuts, tempting fate this way. I wonder—I wonder if my aura's come back?"

"What a strange thing to say," McCleod remarked. "I was just thinking along the same lines. Look, Carey, what can this aura possibly *be*, anyhow? If it's a form of caution, and her touch removed it, it certainly explains your behavior up till now; yet she warned you that death would come from a quarter where you least expected it— Suppose that that was your undoing, in itself?"

"I don't get you, Pete?" Carey said slowly.

"I mean that by telling you it would be *un*expected, you did not therefore fear death in *expected* places. In that way, you might just be ripped to shreds by a lion that you weren't expecting to be a menace."

Carey turned pale. "But that's— That's horrible, Pete! If I can't expect death in the normal danger-places, or even expect it in the normally safe places, then it can come from anywhere, can't it?" He began to mumble fearfully to himself.

"Yes," McCleod said somberly. "It can... *Still* don't like the idea of the rest home, Carey?"

Carey swallowed with difficulty, then sank back against the cushion. "Better give the driver the address, Pete."

"Yes. Yes, I think I'd better."

McCleod leaned forward and gave the driver the new destination, then sat back beside his companion. "If that touch simply removes normal caution, then it seems to me that all you have to do is exercise *abnormal* caution about your life. You'll probably seem like an advanced case of hypochondria to the staff at the home, but don't let it bother you. *Be* fussy about everything, as much as you like. You won't end up very popular, but you'll end up alive, which is more important."

"I won't even get into a wheelchair without airbrakes," Carey said, jokingly. But neither of them laughed.

On the fifth and last day, Carey was lying between the fresh white sheets of his bed, thumbing idly through a magazine, when he heard the door close. He looked up, assuming it was the nurse, then let the magazine drop from his fingers.

"How did *you* get in here?" he said, his body numb with dread.

The girl smiled. "We have our ways," she said softly.

He noticed with an increase of panic that she was brightly blonde, now, even more lovely than when he'd first met her. "I see you're still employed," he said carefully.

"They were very nice about it," she admitted. "They allow a certain margin for ineptness among beginners. I'm to be let rectify my error."

"H-how?" Carey said, eyeing her warily as she moved closer to the bedside, her feet soundless on the polished tile floor. "What are you going to do?"

"Touch you again," she said. "It will bring your aura back. And then you can be assured of bodily safety for the next four months."

"What if I died now? It'd upset their schedule or something?"

She nodded. "You see, you're needed alive, for a time. Your life will contact and cross other lives during the period remaining to you, and without your influence upon them, a great many *other* schedules would be upset, which in turn—"

"I get it," Carey said sullenly. "My early death would yank the plug on the dike, huh? Well, what about my stay *here?* I've been out of contact with 'other lives' for five days, now. I'd imagine all hell was breaking loose without me."

She shook her head, her long hair swirling and glistening in the sunlight. "No, you would have been here anyhow. The sight of that woman's death would have sent you here, since you'd have realized you were on the wrong bus and have been getting off just behind her. The thought that it might almost have been *you* who were run down would have occasioned a slight nervous collapse, much the same as you had for different reasons."

"So where did they goof, then?" Carey said, puzzled.

"It was my fault. They hadn't expected me to stay on the bus after contacting the woman, hence they did not tally the probability of my meeting you four months early... Here, now, I haven't much time. Hold out your hand."

"No," said Carey, putting both hands beneath the sheet and pulling it halfway onto his chin, preparatory to covering his face if she made a grab in that direction. "I'm not going to die now, nor later, if I can help it. Scram, will you!? Please go out of my life and leave it alone!" Suddenly remembering the signal cord pinned to the sheet near his head, he grabbed the slim plastic tube and pressed the button on its tip. "There! A nurse will be here in a few seconds. You'd better clear out."

The girl stared at him, and seemed to be trying to think.

"No, you don't!" he said harshly. "I know what you're on the brink of doing, but forget it! A quick dive at me won't help. I can jump the other way and race around the bed as long as you can, sister!"

His ears were straining for the efficient click of a nurse's white oxfords in the hall outside as he spoke. He could tell the girl was listening, too, as anxious as he was.

"You fool!" she said. "I'm offering you four months of *life!*"

"Don't play semantics with me," Carey spat. "All you're trying to do is guarantee my death! Well, I won't let you. And you can't let me die now, either, or it'll louse up your precious schedule!"

"The schedule has been altered before," she said, her voice flat and hopeless. "It can be again. If you insist on dying today, then I suppose I'll have to let you."

Carey felt a sudden pang. "Look, kid, I hate to bollix up your *job,* but this is my *life* I'm fighting for, remember?"

Her shoulders slumped. "I can't really say I blame you," she said, her voice barely a whisper.

"No hard feelings?" Carey said, hopefully.

She smiled, her face lighting up with forgiveness. "None," she said, and held out her hand.

Carey was within an inch of shaking it, a purely reflex action, when the door opened, and the floor nurse walked in. He yanked his extended fingers away as though they'd been burnt, and rage flooded his soul, as the girl's smile blossomed into a mocking laugh of near-triumph.

"Get out of here!" he roared. "Murderess! Leave me alone!"

The girl didn't move, but the floor nurse did, quickly. The door slammed behind her.

"What—?" said Carey, sitting up, bewildered.

"She can't see me," the girl smiled. "She thought you were talking to her. This means heavy sedation for you, possibly a straitjacket. You're listed with the dangerous cases, you know."

Carey came bolt upright on the bed. "You're nuts!" he said. "Pete knows why I'm here—"

"Your friend Doctor McCleod," the girl said, with a cunning smile, "thinks you're hopelessly insane. Or didn't you know that?"

"They can't do that to me!" Carey said, flipping aside the sheet and striding for the door in his pajamas. "I won't be pinned into one of those canvas horrors. I can't stand being tied up, I—"

"I know," the girl said wearily. "As a child, you were bound by some playmates, and left tied to a tree in the park. You were there all night before your parents and the police found you. You haven't been able to bear being trussed up since then. You don't even wear a belt with your pants. In fact, your pajama bottoms are the type that snap shut, and have no drawstring..."

Carey was still staring at her when the nurse burst in the room with two brawny interns, and subdued him.

By eight that evening, the sedative had worn off, and he began to plead with the girl at his bedside to touch him. He was going mad in that jacket, with his arms lashed crosswise upon his chest. "All right, you've won!" he cried, piteously, while staff members passing in the hall shook their heads solemnly and didn't pause to look in on the man they believed was an incurable maniac.

"Give me the extra four months," Carey pleaded, rolling violently back and forth on the bed, unable to go beyond the padded grip of the leather ankle-straps, which bound his feet to the bedstead. "Go on, touch me, please, I can't stand this. I'm going crazy, you've got to let me out of here, you've got to, you've got to..."

"The schedule," said the girl, sadly, "has already been adjusted, to compensate for your early death, Mister Philips."

"Please, *please!*" he shrieked. "One touch, please! I can't *breathe* in this thing, it's choking me. It's on too tight!"

"Yes," the girl nodded. "It *is* on too tight. You *are* being choked to death."

"Touch me, touch me, *touch me!*" he raved.

At eleven-twenty that night, she finally touched him. But it was merely to close his cold eyelids over his fear-filled sightless eyes.

THE END

OPEN WITH CARE

By Boyd Correll

What woman hasn't claimed to see through her husband for one reason or another? In the case of Emily Staub this was no idle boast.

EMILY STAUB peered closer at her husband. It seemed to her that he was becoming transparent. She could see the dancing flames of the fireplace through him, or at least through part of him.

Her husband, preoccupied with his own thoughts, was not even conscious of her presence. Since leaving the Commission, his mind was on his experiments to the exclusion of everything else, including his wife. His forced retirement had changed him.

Dr. Andrew Staub had participated in the first nuclear experiments when he was only twenty-seven. Because of his age, his genius was not publicized, public opinion being what it was at that time, the government feared to let the people know that such youth had a hand in the then awe-inspiring and fearful development.

Of course, when World War III came along in 1965, Dr. Staub had reached the more mature age of forty-seven. He was duly recognized and acclaimed for his discovery of control of the mutational effects of the progeny of human beings exposed to radioactive blasts. In fact the Commission—though never the Army, Navy, or Air Force—gave direct credit to him for winning World War III. The enemy, their intelligence having ferreted out the fact that we could control the physical and mental make-up of their next generations, decided to throw in the towel. Even the ambitious, live-for-the-moment generals, could not face the prospects of their children or grandchildren making their earthly debut in the shape of jellyfish with the mentalities of univalves.

Dr. Staub was not especially impressed by this outstanding achievement. His main interest was in isotopes. He had a theory, and his wartime accomplishment was merely a primary step towards its perfection. He called this project his Great Experiment and revealed it to no one. It was based on the fact that isotopes are almost identical with the original element.

So for two more decades Dr. Staub raced into new discoveries, which pleased the Commission greatly until he let drop to a colleague that he was nearing the key to mutation of the present generation by the use of isotopes made from certain fissionable elements and properly applied to a fellow human being.

This information, reaching the Top, quickly called for a secret meeting for consideration of when the course of certain things should be brought to a halt. The prospects of Staub's latest enterprise had about the same frightening effect on them as his earlier one had had on the enemy during World War III. It was hastily decided to retire the Commission's greatest scientist.

SO Dr. Staub was put to pasture with proper decorations, a staggeringly generous pension, an ultimatum that he was not to experiment on his fellow human beings, and a thinly veiled suggestion that he turn his efforts towards horticulture or the raising of turkeys. Dr. Staub did not care for the suggestion, accepted the pension, bowed to the ultimatum, and proceeded to build himself a laboratory on his country estate where he could do as he pleased. It was not necessary for him to continue on the mutation of the present generation project because, during this research, he had learned what he needed to further his progress toward the Great Experiment.

But this story is about Emily Staub, the doctor's wife. Emily was thirty years younger than her husband and, because his was strictly a scientific mind, which never entered the realm of society and very seldom that of domestic biology, lived a rather sad and lonely life.

Eighty now, and a complete recluse, Staub spent practically all his waking hours in the laboratory. When he did come into his home fairly early in the evening he usually went directly to his study at the rear of the house—a room forbidden to Emily except to clean; he not trusting any servants within this ivory tower of his.

For the past few years, being so completely absorbed in his Great Experiment, he had rarely spoken to his wife except at mealtime when, for instance, he could not reach the salt.

Emily, long resigned to this strange man whose mind was so full of scientific formulae that to break through his continuous concentration was next to impossible, turned her thoughts inward for contemplation very much as certain Tibetans allegedly stare at their navels. She actually sought desperately for some ailment on which she might concentrate and find diversion. And also, perhaps if she suffered an illness it might throw some of her husband's thoughts toward her.

But she was remarkably healthy for a woman of fifty. Not even a skip in her heartbeat, which could give her an excuse for checking her pulse during his presence. Nor could she discover any aches, pains, or even nerve twinges to think about and wonder if they were indicative of more serious affliction elsewhere within her system. As a hypochondriac she was a failure until Dr. Staub began bringing home the packages.

HE brought home one a week; where from, she did not know, but they must have been from his laboratory for that was his world from which he never wandered. The packages were never the same sizes, and they were wrapped in heavy brown paper. Staub would go straight to his study with these and there he would leave them. A day or so later they would disappear. Although Emily knew quite well that she was to touch nothing in the sacred study, Staub broke his usual silence long enough to warn her when he brought in the first one that they were not to be moved, lifted, or even dusted. He seemed strangely excited.

This almost unprecedented bow of words touched Emily deeply and her eyes clouded momentarily from sheer joy. It was then that she discovered, or thought she discovered, something peculiar about her sight. She wiped away the tears quickly and blinked but still there seemed a cloudy vision. It was when her husband walked between her and the open fireplace that she noticed the apparent illusion—she could see through his left foot!

She heard herself giggle, and was startled by the rather idiotic sound. It must have been provoked by subconscious happiness at finding something wrong with herself, something, which might give her time-consuming thought during the long days.

At dinner Staub's feet were concealed beneath the table so Emily concentrated her efforts to prove that perhaps she was going blind by squinting sharply at objects in the room, closing one eye and then the other until anyone more perceptive than Staub would have noticed and concluded the poor woman was either afflicted with a nervous tic or had become addicted to narcotics.

But Emily now was happy. That night she lay in bed with her bedside light on and stared at the ceiling and the chairs and the curtains so intently that at last she felt a dull pain in the back of her head, which proved conclusively, to her, that some disease was attacking her eyes. For a physicist's wife she sadly lacked scientific or medical knowledge and the only malady she knew of which effected sight was glaucoma. She remembered, as a small girl, her mother telling her about an aunt who had glaucoma. The first noticeable manifestation, she recalled, was that the eyeballs become hard.

Tentatively, Emily pushed on the closed lid of one eye. It did feel hard, giving very little to the pressure, and she tried the other eye. Both seemed to possess the same lack of elasticity. Emily opened her eyes and the room was a blur for a few moments. A bad sign, she was sure. She wished she had someone with whom she could compare the hardness of her eyes. Her husband was in his study, but she did not dare disturb him. She thought of the cat, and slipped out of bed and into the sitting room.

POLYGAMOUS sat before the dying fire sleeping softly, a gentle purr ruffling his throat. He was really Dr. Staub's cat, spending more time at the laboratory than at home. Emily approached him gently. With one finger she pressed against her own eye for comparison, then reached down and pushed against one of Polygamous's closed eyes. Polygamous came awake with a start and backed off indignantly from the probing finger. He almost backed into the fire until he became oriented and that was when Emily noticed that she appeared to see through *him*.

That settled it. Something was definitely wrong. Excitedly hugging her now proven ailment to her bosom, Emily went back into her bedroom, not seeing her husband standing in the shadows of the hallway observing her thoughtfully between narrowing eyes. When she closed her door he gathered up Polygamous and carried him to his study.

Emily slept and was neither conscious of, nor disturbed by, the dull thudding of a pick digging in the garden behind the house.

As the weeks passed Emily became more and more absorbed in her condition, but the novelty and diversion it gave her were now changing to concern. Though she would not at first admit it, she was becoming somewhat frightened. Pushing against her eyes periodically throughout the day to check their hardness naturally developed a functional disorder, and half the time she was either seeing double or conscious of different colored light-rings around objects. And along with these phenomena her husband's anatomy apparently became more and more transparent.

Starting with the left foot, this transparency spread to the right, and then up both legs. At the end of seven weeks she was somewhat shaken to note that, with the exception of Dr. Staub's head, she could see completely through him when he passed between her and a strong light and, more disconcerting still, he would practically disappear from sight when he sat in a darkened part of the room.

Emily went to an oculist.

In his examination room she described her symptoms. The doctor raised an eyebrow.

"You actually see through your husband?" he inquired.

"Oh, yes," said Emily. "And the cat, too—" With a start she realized that she had not seen Polygamous since the night she attempted to check her eyes with his.

"H-m-m-m," said the Doctor. He turned on a bright light and stood in front of it. "Do you—ah—see through me, Mrs. Staub?"

Emily stared hard at the oculist, trying to shake off a chill that had suddenly possessed her. "No," she said. "No. But there seems to be a double outline around you—as though you were standing in two different places."

"I see," said the Doctor. "Ah—how far apart am I?"

"Oh, just a fraction of an inch. More like a wavery line around a light through a foggy window."

HE pushed back her head and examined her eyes closely, a pencil of light from an instrument on his forehead blinding her.

"Do you rub your eyes much, Mrs. Staub?"

"Rub? No. That is, I have been pushing against them with my fingers, checking them for hardness."

"Often?"

"Oh, yes. All through the day," said Emily. "Would that cause things to seem transparent?"

"No," said the Doctor firmly. "But it would cause distortion." He wiggled a finger about even with her ear and some inches from her head. "Do you see that?" he asked.

Emily nodded. "You're wiggling your fingers."

"You haven't got glaucoma. It starts by effecting side vision, and yours is perfect. I'd suggest you stop worrying and also stop pushing your eyes..." He looked at her shrewdly. "And I would like to see Dr. Staub."

"Oh, he doesn't see anybody," said Emily. "Not since he left the Commission."

"He has no assistants in his laboratory?"

"No. We don't even have servants in the house. My husband doesn't trust them."

The oculist decided that he wanted to be done with the Staubs. He was no psychiatrist. He escorted Emily to the door, repeated his advice against worry and rubbing, and bowed her out. When he was gone he went to a shelf and took down a Who's Who and looked up "Staub, Andrew—nuclear scientist" and discovered he had been retired from Government work in 1991.

"A good thing," thought the Doctor. He poured himself a drink.

IT was after midnight of Saturday, the end of the eighth week since the first package was brought in by Dr. Staub. A touch of joy had been brought into her life a few weeks ago on her birthday. She had found on the breakfast table a velvet jeweler's box in which were an exquisite pair of diamond earrings and a matching pendant. Beneath the box was a card on which Dr. Staub had written, "A Happy Birthday—Andrew."

Emily had cried a little and had put on the jewelry and never taken it off. On very depressing days she would touch her ears and fondle the pendant around her neck. She was fondling the pendant this Saturday night in bed as she lay there, unable to sleep. She had not seen her husband since her visit to the oculist, though there were signs each morning that he had come into the house, apparently leaving before she awoke.

Tonight she was determined to make sure her ailment was imaginary. Her hand reached from the pendant to push against an eye, but she jerked it down. The oculist had convinced her that this constant irritation had caused her blurred vision. Since she had stopped this habit things seemed normal again: nothing appeared transparent, which shouldn't be transparent. If only she could catch a glimpse of Polygamous or the doctor it would prove... ʻ

She heard the front door open and she quickly slipped out of bed and went to the door of her room and peered through the slight opening she had left into the living room. The light in the far corner was the only one burning—she always left it for her husband's convenience and he would turn it out on retiring. That was one of the definite signs that he had been coming home nights: the light was always off in the morning.

As she looked through the crack, a wispy blur swept past—a blur so slight and intangible that she was not at all sure there had been one. But watching, she saw the outline of her husband going towards the light. And now he was completely transparent, his figure, except for his head, disappearing entirely for a moment as he walked around the lamp. In his hand he carried the eighth package; a square parcel wrapped in brown paper. It seemed to float through the air, then all movement vanished and blackness took over as the light snapped off. Soft footsteps sounded across the floor and towards the study.

Emily crept back into bed, bewildered, and with an odd weakness. She could not sleep and was up earlier than usual the next morning. She knew Dr. Staub had not left because she would have heard the door open and close. And, lying awake, she had half convinced herself that the shadows of night had merely caused another illusion; the oculist had been *so* convincing.

She waited patiently but Staub did not come from his study.

AT eleven-thirty she bravely walked to his quarters: a bedroom and dressing room connected with the study. She peered into the bedroom and at the bed, but the blinds were closed and the room almost in darkness. She allowed her eyes to become accustomed to the gloom and studied the bed. She could see no one there yet there was an indentation the shape of a human's body, and the bedclothes were strangely piled up as though covering a figure. The head of the figure could easily be hidden by a large, pushed-aside pillow.

The odd weakness, accompanied by fear, rose in her again and she felt panic. She turned and went swiftly through the back door and into her garden. She hadn't been in the garden for many days.

A hundred feet from the study window, shaded by a live oak tree, was a bed of tuberous begonias and to her dismay a mongrel dog was digging furiously in the center of it. For a moment she forgot her fear and shouted at the dog who stopped his digging and ran.

Emily approached to see the extent of damage to her flowers when she saw, at the bottom of the hole, a mass of fur, and less exposed, a smaller mass. She probed the exposed fur with a stick and disclosed the body of Polygamous. A nauseating odor assailed her nostrils and swept away her first feeling of pity for the cat as well as concern for Dr. Staub who was so fond of Polygamous. Ill, she started back into the house when she noticed seven empty cartons and balled wads of brown paper shoved deep into the huge wood-box by the door. The paper was of the same type that covered the packages. Had Dr. Staub accidentally killed the cat and brought it home in a carton and then buried it? Then what had been in the other packages? Other animals? Dead animals her husband may have destroyed in experiments and also buried? She remembered the odd sizes—one box had been especially large, large enough to contain a shepherd dog.

For a long time she sat in the living room, watching the door to her husband's suite. She had left it slightly ajar when she made her hasty exit and through this opening she could see the foot of his bed. In the dimness of the room she thought she saw a light movement there, but it was so quick she could not be sure. Then, only moments later, something soft pressed against her leg. She managed not to scream and looked down.

Very faintly the outline of Polygamous brushed against the chair, glided to the fireplace.

EMILY closed her eyes against a darkness, which pushed around her. The darkness passed and an irresistible force drew her to the partly opened door. She had to see what was in the eighth package.

She crept past the disordered bed and into the study and up to the library table. On it was the square parcel she had seen the night before, and over it she could see into the bedroom.

She reached for the box, still watching the bed. She unfolded the brown paper, trying to hush the rustling noise. The carton inside was of considerable weight and thumped as she turned it over.

There was violent movement in the bed. The covers were thrown back and the window shade lifted. Against the light she clearly saw Dr. Staub's head as he rose to glare at her.

Then his glare turned to a monstrous grin of victory. He leapt to his feet in the bed and bounced like a schoolboy except that his head was like a pumpkin on a string with no body to support it.

In a hoarse whisper that was like a shout he said to the ceiling:

"It works! It works! The pendant properly applied the isotopes! The whole body can live!"

His dangling head, his insane grin, the bed responding in jerks to no visible force was too terrifying for Emily to watch and she dropped her gaze to the box her fingers had automatically opened.

Inside the box was her own head.

THE END

If you've enjoyed this book, you will not want to miss these terrific titles…

ARMCHAIR SCI-FI & HORROR DOUBLE NOVELS, $12.95 each

D-71   **THE DEEP END** by Gregory Luce
TO WATCH BY NIGHT by Robert Moore Williams

D-72   **SWORDSMAN OF LOST TERRA** by Poul Anderson
PLANET OF GHOSTS by David V. Reed

D-73   **MOON OF BATTLE** by J. J. Allerton
THE MUTANT WEAPON by Murray Leinster

D-74   **OLD SPACEMEN NEVER DIE!** John Jakes
RETURN TO EARTH by Bryan Berry

D-75   **THE THING FROM UNDERNEATH** by Milton Lesser
OPERATION INTERSTELLAR by George O. Smith

D-76   **THE BURNING WORLD** by Algis Budrys
FOREVER IS TOO LONG by Chester S. Geier

D-77   **THE COSMIC JUNKMAN** by Rog Phillips
THE ULTIMATE WEAPON by John W. Campbell

D-78   **THE TIES OF EARTH** by James H. Schmitz
CUE FOR QUIET by Thomas L. Sherred

D-79   **SECRET OF THE MARTIANS** by Paul W. Fairman
THE VARIABLE MAN by Philip K. Dick

D-80   **THE GREEN GIRL** by Jack Williamson
THE ROBOT PERIL by Don Wilcox

ARMCHAIR SCIENCE FICTION CLASSICS, $12.95 each

C-25   **THE STAR KINGS**
by Edmond Hamilton

C-26   **NOT IN SOLITUDE**
by Kenneth Gantz

C-32   **PROMETHEUS II**
by S. J. Byrne

ARMCHAIR SCI-FI & HORROR GEMS SERIES, $12.95 each

G-7   **SCIENCE FICTION GEMS, Vol. Four**
Jack Sharkey and others

G-8   **HORROR GEMS, Vol. Four**
Seabury Quinn and others

If you've enjoyed this book, you will not want to miss these terrific titles…